Nellie Bly

The Mystery of Central park

A Novel

Nellie Bly

The Mystery of Central park
A Novel

ISBN/EAN: 9783337043230

Printed in Europe, USA, Canada, Australia, Japan

Cover: Foto ©Andreas Hilbeck / pixelio.de

More available books at **www.hansebooks.com**

THE

MYSTERY

OF

CENTRAL PARK.

A Novel.

BY

NELLIE BLY,

AUTHOR OF

"TEN DAYS IN A MAD HOUSE" AND "SIX MONTHS
IN MEXICO."

NEW YORK:

· COPYRIGHT, 1889, BY

G. W. Dillingham, Publisher,

SUCCESSOR TO G. W. CARLETON & Co.

MDCCCLXXXIX.

Trow's
Printing and Book Binding Co.,
N. Y.

CONTENTS.

Chapter		Page
I.	The Young Girl on the Bench..........	7
II.	Penelope Sets a Hard Task for Dick	19
III.	Wherein Dick Treadwell Meets with Another Adventure.....................	45
IV.	Story of the Girl who Attempted Suicide .	64
V.	The Failure of the Strike	77
VI.	Is the Girl Honest?	87
VII.	Mr. Martin Shanks : Guardian	95
VIII.	The Missing Stenographer..............	103
IX.	The Stranger at the Bar................	114
X.	Tolman Bike	121
XI.	Who was the Man that Bought the Gown ?	139
XII.	One and the Same	153
XIII.	A Lovers' Quarrel.....................	166

Chapter		Page
XIV.	"Give Me Until To-Morrow."	177
XV.	"To Richard Treadwell, Personal."	190
XVI.	The Mystery Solved	205
XVII.	Sunlight Through the Clouds	220

THE
MYSTERY OF CENTRAL PARK.

CHAPTER I.

THE YOUNG GIRL ON THE BENCH.

" And that is your final decision ?"

Dick Treadwell gazed sternly at Penelope Howard's downcast face, and waited for a reply.

Instead of answering, as good-mannered young women generally do, Penelope intently watched the tips of her russet shoes, as they appeared and disappeared beneath the edge of her gown, and remained silent.

[7] .

When she raised her head and met that look, so sad and yet so stern, the faintest shadow of a smile placed a pleasing wrinkle at the corners of her brown eyes.

"Yes, that is — my final decision," she repeated, slowly.

Dick Treadwell dropped despondently on a bench and, gazing steadily over the green lawn, tried to think it all out.

He felt that he was not being used quite fairly, but he was at a loss for a way to remedy it.

Here he was, the devoted slave of the rather plain girl beside him, who refused to marry him, merely because he had never soiled his firm, white hands with toil, nor worried his brain with a greater task, since his school days, than planning some way to kill time.

He was one of those unfortunate mortals possessed of an indolent disposition, and had been left a modest legacy, that, though making him far from wealthy, was still enough to support him in idleness.

He lacked the spur of necessity which urged men on to greater deeds.

In short, Richard was one of those worthless ornaments of society that live, and die without doing much good or any great harm.

That he was an ornament, however, none dared to deny, and the expressive brown eyes of the girl, who had seated herself beside him bore ample testimony that she was not unconscious of his manly charms.

Dick took off his straw hat, and after running his firm, white fingers through his kinky, light hair, crossed one leg over the other, while he brooded moodily on his peculiar fate. The frank, boyish expression, that had won him so many admirers, was displaced by a heavy frown, and his bright blue eyes gazed unseeingly over the beautiful vista before him.

He could not understand why a girl should get such crazy ideas, any way. There were plenty of girls who made no effort to hide their admiration for him, and he knew that they could be had for the asking, if it only wasn't for Penelope.

But, somehow, Penelope had more attraction for him than any girl he had ever met. Her very obstinacy, her independence, made her all the more charming to him, even if it was provoking.

Penelope Howard was in no wise Dick Treadwell's mate in beauty.

She was slender to boniness and tall, but willowy and graceful, and one forgot her murky complexion when gazing into the depths of her bright, expressive eyes and catching the curve of a wonderfully winsome smile.

Penelope was an heiress, though, to a million dollars or more, and so no one ever called her plain.

She was an orphan and had been reared by a sensible old aunt, who would doubtless leave her another million.

Penelope knew her defects as well and better than did other people. Shd had no vanity and was blessed with an unusual amount of solid sense.

Penelope Howard was well aware that she would not have to go begging for a husband, but she had loved handsome Dick Treadwell ever since the year before she graduated at Vassar. He had gone there to pay his devotions to another fair under-graduate and came away head over heels in love with Penelope. Nevertheless Penelope was in no hurry to marry.

She loved Richard with all her heart, but there was a barrier between them which he alone could remove.

"You know, Dick," she said, softly, as he still gazed across the green lawn, trying to find a mental foothold, as it were, "that I told you this before"——

"Yes, this makes the sixth time I have proposed," he said, savagely, still looking away.

"I have always told you," smiling slightly at his remark and lowering her voice as she glanced apprehensively at a girl seated on a bench near by, "that I will not marry you as long as you live as you do. I have money enough for two, so it makes no difference whether the man I marry has any or not. But I can't and won't marry a—a worthless man— one who has never done anything, and is too indolent to do anything. I want a husband who has some ability—who has accomplished something—just one worthy thing even, and then—well, it won't make so much difference if he is indolent afterwards. You know, Dick, how much I care for you," softly, "how fond I am of you, but I will not marry you until you prove that you are able to do something."

"It's all very easy to talk about," he replied savagely, "but what can I do? I don't dare risk what little I have in Wall street. I don't know enough to preach, or to be a doctor, or a lawyer, and it takes too infernally long to go back to the beginning and learn. You object to my following the races, and I couldn't sell ribbons or run a hotel to save me. Tell me what to do, Penelope, and I will gladly make the attempt. When you took a —a craze to walk in the Park at a hideous hour every morning before your friends, who don't think it good form, were out to frown you down, did I not promise to be your escort, and haven't I faithfully got up—or stayed up —to keep my promise?"

"And only late — let us see how many times?" she asked roguishly.

"Penelope, don't," he pleaded. "You know I love you. Why, Penel', love, if I thought that your foolish whim would separate us forever I'd—— Oh, darling, you don't doubt my love, do you?'

"Hush!" she whispered, warningly, pointing to the girl on the other bench.

"Oh, she is asleep," Dick replied carelessly.

"Don't he too sure," Penelope urged, gazing abstractedly towards the girl, her eyes soft with the feeling that was thrilling her heart.

Like all girls Penelope never tired of hearing the man who had won her love swearing his devotion, but like all girls she preferred to be the sole and only listener to those vows, to that tone.

"If she is awake she is the first young woman I ever saw who would let her new La Tosca sunshade lie on the ground," he said laughingly.

"She must be sleeping," Penelope assented indifferently, glancing at the parasol lying in the dust where it had apparently rolled from the girl's knee.

Two gray squirrels, with their bushy tails held stiffly erect, came out on the dusty drive, and finding everything quiet scampered across to the green sward, where they stood upright in the green grass viewing curiously the un-happy lovers.

Penelope had a mania for carrying peanuts to the Park to give to the animals. She took several from her reticule and tossed them to-wards the gray squirrels.

The one, with a little whistling noise scam-pered up the nearest tree and the other, tak-ing a nut in his little mouth, quickly followed.

"I have not seen her move since we came here," she said, returning to the subject of the girl. "Do you suppose she put her hat over her eyes in that manner to keep the light out of them, or was it done to keep any passers-by from staring at her?"

"I don't know," carelessly. "Probably she is ill."

"Ill? Do you think so, Dick? I am going to speak to her, declared Penelope, impulsively.

"Don't, I wouldn't," urged Dick.

"But I will," declared Penelope.

"You don't know anything about her," he continued pleadingly. She may have been out all night, or you can't tell but perhaps she has been drinking too much, and if you wake her she will doubtless make it unpleasant for you."

"How uncharitable you are," indignantly exclaimed Penelope, who feared no one. She had spent much time and money in doing deeds of charity, and she had met all sorts and conditions of women. That a woman was in trouble and she could help her, was all Penelope cared to know.

She got up and walked towards the girl. Richard, knowing all argument was useless, went with her. When they stopped, Penelope, bending down, peeped beneath the brim of the lace hat which, laden with an abundance of red roses, was tilted over the motionless girl's face.

"She is sleeping," she whispered softly to Dick. "Her eyes are closed. She has a lovely face."

"Has she, indeed?" and Dick, with increased interest, bent to look. "She is very pale and—I am afraid that she is ill," in an awed tone. "Young lady!" he called nerviously,

The girlish figure never moved. Richard's and Penelope's eyes met with a swift expression—a mingled look of surprise and fear.

"My dear!" called Penelope, gently shaking the girl by the shoulder.

The lace hat tumbled off and lay at their

feet; the little hands, which had been folded loosely in her lap, fell apart and the girlish figure fell lengthwise on the bench.

Breathlessly and silently the frightened young couple looked at the beautiful up-turned face framed in masses of golden hair; the blue-rimmed eyes, with their curly dark lashes resting gently against the colorless skin; the parted lips in which there lingered a bit of red.

Nervously Richard touched the cheek of pallor, and felt for the heart and pulse.

"What's wrong there?" called a gray-uni-formed officer, who had left his horse near the edge of the walk.

Penelope silently looked at Richard, waiting for him to answer, and as he raised his face all white and horror-stricken, he gasped:

"My God! The girl is dead."

CHAPTER II.

PENELOPE SETS A HARD TASK FOR DICK.

Richard Treadwell was not mistaken.

The golden-haired girl was dead.

The fair young form was taken to the Morgue, and for some days the newspapers were filled with accounts of the mystery of Central Park, and everybody was discussing the strange case.

And what could have been more mysterious?

A young and exquisitely beautiful girl, clad in garments stylish and expensive, although quiet in tone, and such as women of refinement wear, found dead on a bench in Central Park by two young people, whose social position was in those circles where to be

brought in any way to public notice is considered almost a disgrace.

And to add to the mystery of the case the
most thorough examination of the girl's body
had failed to show the slightest wound or dis-
coloration, or the faintest clue to the cause of
the girl's death.

The newspapers had all their own theories.
Some were firm in their belief of foul play,
but they could not even hint at the cause of
death, and how such a lovely creature could
have been murdered, if murder it was, in
Central Park and the assassin or assassins
escape unseen, were riddles they could not
solve.

Other journals hooted at the idea of foul
play. They claimed the girl had, while walking in Central Park, sat down on the bench,
and died either of heart disease or of poison
administered by her own hand.

The police authorities maintained an air of

impenetrable secrecy, but promised that within a few days they would furnish some startling developments. They did not commit them-. selves, however, as to their ideas of how the girl met her death. In this they were wise, for the silent man is always credited with knowing a great deal more than the man does who talks, and so the public waited impatiently from day to day, confident the police would soon clear the mystery away.

Hundreds of people visited the Morgue, curious to look upon the dead girl.

Many went there in search of missing friends, hoping and yet dreading that in the mysterious dead girl they would find the one for whom they searched.

People from afar telegraphed for the body to be held until their arrival, but they came and went and the beautiful dead girl was still unidentified.

Penelope Howard and Richard Treadwell

were made to figure prominently in all the
stories about the beautiful mystery, much to
their discomfort.   The untiring reporters
called to see Penelope at all hours, whenever a
fresh theory gave them an excuse to drag her
name before the public again, and poor
Richard had no peace at his club, at his rooms,
or at Penelope's home.   If the reporters were
not interviewing him, his friends were asking
all manner of questions concerning the strange
affair, and pleading repeatedly for the story of
the discovery of the body to be told again.
Some of his club acquaintances even went
so far as to joke him about the girl he had
found dead, and there was much quiet smiling
among his immediate friends at Dick's fondness
for early walks, a trait first brought to light by
his connection with this now celebrated case.

Not the least important figure in the sensation was the Park policeman who found
Penelope and Richard bending over the dead

girl. He became a very great personage all at once. The meritorious deeds which marked his previous record were the finding of a lost child and the frantically chasing a stray dog, which he imagined was mad, and wildly firing at it—very wide of the mark, it is true—until the poor frightened little thing disappeared in some remote corner.

This officer became the envy of the Park policemen. Daily his name appeared in connection with the case as "the brave officer of the 'Mystery of Central Park.'" Daily he was pointed out by the people, who thronged to the spot where the girl was found, curious to see the bench and to carry away with them some little memento. He always managed to be near the scene of the mystery during the busy hours of the Park, and the dignity with which he answered questions as to the exact bench, was very impressive.

But the officer's pride at being connected

with such a sensational case was not to be wondered at.

Rarely had New York been so stirred to its depth over a mysterious death. The newspapers published the most minute descriptions of the dead girl's dainty silk underwear, of her exquisitely made Directoire dress, of her Suede shoes, the silver handled La Tosca sunshade, and more particularly did they dwell on descriptions of her dainty feet and tiny hands, of her perfect features and masses of beautiful yellow hair.

There was every indication of refinement and luxury about her.

How came it, then, that a being of such beauty and grace could have no one who missed her; could have no one to search frantically the wide world for her?

The day of the inquest came.

Penelope, accompanied by her aunt and Richard, were forced to be present. Penelope in a very steady voice told how they found the body, and she was questioned and cross-questioned as to the reason why she should have become so interested in the sight of an apparently sleeping girl as to accost her.

It was a most unusual thing.

Did she not think that it had been sug-gested by the young man who accompanied her ?

Penelope's cheeks burned and she became very indignant at their efforts to connect Richard more closely with the case, and she related all that had transpired after they spoke of the girl with such minuteness and ease, that it was hinted afterwards that she had studied the story in order to protect the culprit.

Poor Richard came next.

His story did not differ from Penelope's, and while no one said in so many words that they suspected him of knowing more than he divulged, yet he felt their suspicions and accusations in every question and every look.

A very knowing newspaper had that same morning published a long story, relating instances where murderers could not remain away from their victims, and always returned to the spot, in many cases pretending to be the discoverer of the murder. The story finished by demanding that the authorities decide at the inquest whose hand was in the murder of the beautiful young girl.

Dick, remembering all this, felt his heart swell with indignation at the tones of his examiner.

Penelope was more indignant, if anything, than Dick, but she had read in a newspaper that repudiated the theory of murder, a collection of accounts of deaths which had been thought suspicious that were afterwards proven to be the result of heart disease or poison, and she quietly hoped that the doctors who held the post-mortem examination would set at rest all the doubts in the case.

The park policeman, in a grandiloquent manner, gave his testimony.

He told how he found the young couple bending over the dead girl, who was half lying on a bench. When the officer asked what was wrong, the young man, who seemed excited and frightened—and he laid great stress on those words—replied " The girl is dead." The officer had then looked at the body but did not touch it. The young people denied any knowledge of the girl's identity, and then his suspicions being aroused he asked the young man why he had replied " The girl is dead," if he did not know her?

The young man repeated that he had never seen the dead girl before, and his companion gave him a quick, frightened glance ; so the officer said sternly :

"Be careful, young man, remember you are talking to the law; I'll have to report everything you say."

And then the officer paused to take breath and at the same time to give proper weight to his words. Everybody took the opportunity to remove their gaze from the officer and to see how Dick Treadwell was bearing it. They were getting more interested now and nearly everyone felt that the elegant young man would be in the clutches of the law by the time the inquest was adjourned.

The officer cleared his throat and in a deep, gruff voice continued his story.

At his warning the young man had flushed very red, then paled, and then he called the officer a fool.

Still the conscientious limb of the law determined to know more about two young people, who, while able to drive, were doing such unusual and extraordinary things as walking early in the Park and happening upon the dead body of a young girl ; so he asked the young man why, if he did not know the girl, he did not say "*a* girl is dead here," instead of "*the* girl is dead," whereupon the young man told the officer again that he was a fool, adding several words to make it more emphatic, and at this the young girl, who stood by very gravely up to this time, had the boldness and impudence to laugh.

Richard Treadwell was called again, and had to repeat the reason of his early walk in the Park, and had to tell where he spent the previous evening, which was proven by Penelope and her aunt. He was questioned why he used the definite article instead of the indefinite in answering the officer's question. He could offer no explanation.

That a man should say "*the* girl" instead of "*a* girl," and that he should be excited over finding the body of a girl unknown to him, were things that looked very suspicious to the law, and those in charge of the inquest had no hesitancy in showing the fact.

A few persons whose testimony was unimportant were called, and then came the doctors who had made the post-mortem examination. Nothing was discovered to indicate murder or suicide, nor, indeed, could they come to any definite conclusion as to the cause of death.

The coroner's jury brought in an indefinite verdict, showing that they knew no more about the circumstances or cause of the girl's death than they did at the beginning of the inquest. With this unsatisfactory conclusion the public was forced to rest content.

They did know that the girl had not been shot or stabbed, which was some satisfaction, at any rate.

Penelope persuaded her aunt and Richard to accompany her through the Morgue. She was deeply hurt at the way in which Dick had been treated. Still she wanted to look on the face of the fair young girl, the cause of all the worriment, before she was taken to her grave.

"How dreadful!" exclaimed Penelope's aunt, as the keeper unbolted the door and waited, before he closed it, for them to enter the low room.

She tiptoed daintly over the stone floor— which, wet all over, had little streams formed in places flowing from different hose—holding her skirts up with one hand, and with the other hand held a perfumed handkerchief over her aristocratic nose. Penelope, with serious but calm face, kept close to the keeper, and Richard walked silently with the aunt.

"I thought the bodies lay on marble slabs," said Penelope, glancing at the row of plain, unpainted rough boxes set close together on iron supports.

" They did in the old Morgue, but ever since we've been in this building we put them in the boxes. They keep better this way," explained the keeper, delighted to show the sights of the Morgue to persons of social prominence.

" Do you know the history of all these dead ?" asked Penelope, counting the fifty and odd coffins which came one after the other.

" We know somethin' about most all 'cept those found in the river, and the river furnishes more bodies than the whole city do.   We photograph every body and we pack their clothes away, with a description of 'em, and keep them six months.   The photographs we always keep, so that years after people may find their lost here.   Would you like to see them, miss ?"

" You see," continued the man, lifting a lid, "we burn a cross on the coffins of the Catholics, and the Protestants get no mark.

The boxes with the chalk mark on are the ones that's to be buried to-morrow. This man here, miss," holding the lid up, "was a street-car driver; want to see him, mam?"

Penelope's aunt shook her head negatively.

" He struck, and could not get work after-wards, so as he and his family was starvin', he made them one less by committing suicide."

" It is so hard to die," Penelope said with a shudder.

" Hard? Not a bit, miss; death's a great boon to poor people. This 'ere fellow," hold-ing another lid while Penelope gazed with dry, burning eyes down on a weather-beaten face, which, seared with a million premature wrinkles, wore a smile of rest, "he was a tramp, they 'spose. Fell dead on Sixth Avenue, an' he had nothin' on him to identify him. And this 'ere woman who lies next the Park mystery girl, though she do smile like she got somethin' she wanted—an' they nearly all smile, miss, when they've handed in their 'counts—she were a devil. She's done time on the island, and they've had her in Blackwell's Insane Asylum, but 'twan't no good; soon as she got out she was at her old tricks. Drink, drink, if she had to steal it, an' fight an' swear! They picked her up on a sidewalk the last time and hauled her to the station-house, but when mornin' come an' they called her she didn't show up; an' when they dragged her out, thinkin' she was still full, they found she'd got a death sentence and gone on a last trip to the island where they never come back."

A little woman, stumpy, fat and old, in a shabby black frock and plain black bonnet, came in with one of the keeper's assistants. She held a coarse white cotton handkerchief in her hand, and her wrinkled, broad face with its fish-like mouth, thick, upturned nose and watery blue eyes, looked prepared to show evidence of grief when the search among the labelled rough-boxes was successful.

"Mrs. Lang," read the man who was assisting the woman in her search, "from the Almshouse?"

"Yes, that was her name, true enough. The Lord rest her soul!" the woman responded fervently, and the man slid the lid across the box, and the little old woman, holding the handkerchief over her stubby nose, peeped in.

"Yes, that's her; that's Mrs. Lang. Poor thing! Ah! she do look desolate," she wailed. "She hasn't a fri'nd in all the world," she continued, looking with her weak eyes at Penelope, who sympathetically stopped by her. "She was eighty years old, and paralyzed from her knees down. Poor thing, they took her to the Almshouse not quite a month ago, and she looks like she'd had a hard time, sure enough. Poor Mrs. Lang, she do look desolate."

The man closed the box as if he had given her time enough to weep, and the wailing woman went out.

"What becomes of the bodies of these poor unfortunates?" asked Penelope, with a catch in her voice.

"Most of 'em we give to the medical colleges as subjects. Yes, men and women, black and white alike. That nigger woman, who wouldn't tell on the man who gave her a death stab, lying to the other side of the Park mystery girl, will be taken to a college to-night. The bodies not sold are all sent up to Hart's Island, where they're buried in a big trench."

Penelope's sympathic nature quivered with pity by reason of what she had seen and heard. She secretly resolved to give the poor unknown girl a respectable burial, and to order some flowers to be strewed in the rough-boxes with the other unfortunates who would be taken to the Potter's Field to-morrow.

"Death is a horrible thing," she remarked sadly, as they filed through the iron doors again.

"It is, miss," the keeper assented. "I've had charge of this here Morgue for these twenty years, still if I was to allow myself to think about death and the mystery of the hereafter, I'd go crazy.

"But the thought of Heaven. It is surely some consolation," faltered Penelope.

"Twenty years' work in there," nodding his head towards the throne where death sits always ; where the only noise is the sound of the dripping water ; " hasn't left any fairy tales in my mind about what comes after. We live, and when we're dead that's the last of it. You can tell children about the ' good man ' and ' bad man ' and Heaven and—beggin' your pardon—Hell, just the same as you tell them about Santa Claus, but when they grow up if they thinks for themselves they know its fairy tales—all fairy tales. When you're dead, you're dead, and that's the last of it, take my word for that."

Penelope was not a religious fanatic, but her few pious beliefs experienced a little resentful shock at the man's outspoken words. She haughtily drew her shoulders up, the kind expression faded from her face, leaving it less attractive, and she was conscious of a little feeling of repulsion for the unbelieving Morgue keeper. Not that the keeper's ideas were so foreign to those that had visited her own mind. She had many times felt dubious on such subjects herself, but she had always felt it to be her duty to kill doubt and trust in that which was taught her concerning the life hereafter.

Penelope joined her aunt and Richard Treadwell, where they stood under a shade tree opposite the Morgue waiting her.

In a few words she told what she wished

to do.   Her kind aunt good naturedly encouraged her.   Perhaps what they had seen
had had a softening effect on her as well.

Instead of driving home they drove to the
coroner's, and with the permit which they
obtained without difficulty, to an undertakers,
where the final arrangements were made for
the girl's burial.

So the beautiful mystery of Central Park
was not sent to a medical college nor to the
Potter's Field,   The next morning Penelope
accompanied Richard in his coupé, and Mrs.
Louise Van Brunt, her aunt, who had in her
carriage two charitable old lady friends, followed the sombre hearse in its slow journey
across the bridge to Brooklyn.   In a quiet
graveyard on the outskirts of the city the dead
girl was lowered into the earth.

Penelope was greatly wrought up over the
case.   All the way to the graveyard she was
moody and silent.   Seeing that she was not

inclined to talk, Richard too sat silent and thoughtful.

Added to her interest in the dead girl, the evident suspicions entertained against Richard had preyed upon Penelope's mind. While she never doubted Richard's innocence in the affair, still ugly thoughts concerning his care-less nature, and the recalled rumors of affairs with actresses, of more or less renown, which the newspapers darkly hinted at, almost set her wild. Could it be possible that he had known the girl, or ever seen her before they found her dead?

She recalled his excitement when he leaned · down and for the first time saw the face of the . girl as she sat on the bench. The officer had laid great stress on Dick's excited manner, and to Penelope, as she looked back, it seemed suggestive of more than he had acknowledged.

"And I love him, I love him," she cried to herself during the long ride to the cemetery, "and with this horrible suspicion hanging over him I could never marry him; I could never be happy if I did. I can never be happy if I don't. If we only knew something about it; if only people did not hint things; if I could only crush the horrible idea that he knows more than he told!"

They dismounted, after driving into the cemetery, and walked silently across the green; winding in and out among the grassy and flowered beds and white stones which marked all that had once been life—hope.

An unknown but Christian minister stood waiting them at the open grave. Penelope glanced at him and at the workmen, who left the shade of a tree near-by when they saw the party approaching, and came forward with faces void of any feeling but that of impudent curiosity. The minister repeated the burial service very softly, as the coffin was lowered into the earth. Penelope's throat felt bursting, and her heart beat painfully as Richard, with strangely solemn face, dropped some flowers into the grave.

"Oh death? How horrible, how horrible!" she thought, "and I, too, some day must die; must be put in a grave, and then—and then, what? What have we done to our Creator that we must die? And that poor girl! This is the last for all eternity, and there is not one here she knew to see the last, unless"—— but the morbid thought against Richard refused to form itself into definite shape.

The men who filled the grave were the most light-hearted in the group. They pulled up a board, and the pile of fresh earth at the mouth of the grave, which it had upheld, went rattling in on the coffin and flowers, almost gladly it seemed to Penelope. She shivered slightly, but watched as if fascinated, until the men put on the last shovel-full and with a spade deftly shaped out the mound.

Richard helped her cover the newly-made grave with the flowers and green ivy and smilax they had brought for that purpose.

They were the last to leave. The others had walked slowly among the graves and back to the place where the carriages were waiting. The hearse, immediately after the coffin was lowered into the earth, had gone off with rollicking speed, as if eager for new freight, and the workmen with their spades and picks had disappeared.

"It is ended," said Dick with a relieved sigh, as he led Penelope back to her carriage. "Now let us forget all the misery of these last few days and be happy."

"It is not ended," exclaimed Penelope, spiritedly. "It has only begun. I can never be happy until I know the secret of that girl's death."

"That is impossible, Penelope," replied Dick. "That mystery can never be solved."

"Dick, you have sworn you love me; you have sworn that you would do anything I asked if I would marry you. Did you mean it? Will you swear it again?" cried Penelope, breathlessly.

"Mean it, love?" repeated Dick, as he pressed her hand closely between his arm and heart. "Upon my life, I swear it."

"Then solve the mystery of that girl's death, and I will be your wife."

CHAPTER III.

WHEREIN DICK TREADWELL MEETS WITH ANOTHER ADVENTURE.

Richard Treadwell was in despair. Days had passed since the burial of the unknown girl, and he was no nearer the solution of the mystery than he was on the morning of the discovery. He had not learned one new thing in the case, and what was infinitely worse, he had not the least idea how to set about the task.

He had taken to wandering restlessly about the city racked with the wildest despondency.

"Great Lord, if I only had an idea," he thought, desperately, as he walked up Fifth Avenue. "If I only knew how to begin—if I only knew where to begin—if I only knew what to do—if I only— Confound the girl, anyhow. Why couldn't she have died somewhere else, or why didn't some one else find her instead of us. Confound it, I'll be hanged if I hadn't enough to worry about before. Women will take the most infernal whims. Good Lord! If I wasn't suspected of being connected with her death, and if Penelope—— But I'll be d—— if I can give it the go-by. It's solve the mystery or lose Penelope! If I only knew how to go to work. But, by Jove, I know I could preach a sermon, or set a broken leg, or—or cook a dinner easier than find out why, where, when, how, that yellow-haired girl died. Curse my luck, anyhow."

"I have read stories where fellows who don't know much start out to solve murder mysteries, but they always find something which all the detectives and police authorities overlooked, which gives them the right clue to work on. It's very good for tales, but I find nothing. The rest are just as smart and smarter at finding clues than I am. They got nothing. I got nothing, and what to do would puzzle a Solomon."

Dick stopped and looked up to the windows of Penelope's home, where his wandering feet had brought him. He had not seen her for two days; so busy on the case, he wrote her with a groan, and then he had sent her a bunch of roses, and gone forth to kill another day in aimless wanderings.

But here, before her door—how could a lover resist the temptation to enter and be happy in the presence of his divinity for a few moments at least? Richard was not one of the resisting kind any way, so, after a moment's thought, he ran up the broad stone steps and was ushered into Penelope's room off the library—half sitting-room, half study —to wait for her.

Nothing was wanting in Penelope's special den, that luxury could suggest, to make it an exquisite retreat for a young woman with a taste for the beautiful. There were heavy portieres, soft, rich carpet, handsome rugs here and there on the floor and thrown carelessly over low divans. Chairs and lounges of different shapes, all made for comfort, little tables strewed with rich bric-a-brac, unique spirit lamps, and on easels and hanging around were paintings and etchings, all of which, as Penelope said, had a story in them.

There were some fine statues, among which were several the work of Penelope. A little low organ, with a piano lamp near it, stood open and there were music and books in profusion.

Near where the daylight came strongest was a sensible flat-top desk littered with paper, cards, books and the thousand little trinkets—

useless, if you please—which a refined woman gathers about to please her eye.

The most unusual things that would have impressed a stranger, if by some unknown chance he could gain admittance here, was a mixed collection of odd canes and weapons, and a skull in the centre of the desk, which was utilized as an inkstand and a penholder.

"Why, Dick," said Penelope, as she tripped lightly in, clad in an artistic gray carriage gown. "I am glad to see you. I wish you had been earlier so you could have enjoyed a drive with aunt and me."

"I have been busy," Richard said bravely, releasing the hand she had given him on entering.

They sat down together on a sofa.

"I have been so occupied that I haven't had time for a drive these last few days."

"And have you discovered anything yet?" Penelope asked, eagerly.

"Well, not exactly," hesitatingly, "it will take time to clear it all up, you know."

"Tell me, do you know her name yet, and where she came from, and was she really murdered?"

"Slowly, slowly; would you have me spoil my luck by telling what I have done?" asked Richard evasively, his eyes twinkling.

"Oh, you superstitious boy," laughed Penelope, lightly tapping him with her hand, which he immediately caught and held captive in his own.

"Don't be unkind," he pleaded, as she tried to draw her hand away.

"Not for worlds," she replied gravely, ceasing to struggle. "Mr. John Stetson Maxwell called here last night, and he told me of an experience he had when he was an editor, that made me resolve never to speak or act unkindly if I can help it."

"I am deeply obliged to Mr. Maxwell,"
Richard responded lightly.

"But it was very sad, Dick. I felt unhappy all the evening over it."

"I wish my miseries and wretchedness
could have the same influence on you," he
broke in with a laugh.

"Don't you want to hear the story? I had
intended to tell it to you," she said, half provoked at his lack of seriousness.

"Why, certainly. By all means," he replied, grave enough now. He never joked
when she assumed that tone and look.

"When he was an editor," she began softly,
"he one day received a very bright poem from
a man in Buffalo. He did not know the man
as a writer, still the poem was so meritorious
that he straightway accepted it, and sent a
note to the author enclosing a check for the
work. A few days afterwards, the man's card
was sent in, with a request for an interview.

Mr. Maxwell was very busy at the time, but he thought he would give the man a moment, so he told the boy to bring the visitor up. When he came in, Mr. Maxwell was surprised to see a young man of some twenty-five years. He was not well clad, and was much abashed when he found himself in the presence of such a great personage as the editor, Mr. Maxwell."

"Rightly, rightly," Richard said, good naturedly, patting her hands encouragingly.

"Mr. Maxwell recalled afterwards that the young man looked in wretched spirits," Penelope continued, with a slow smile. "At the time he was too hurried to notice anything, and then editors are used to seeing people who are in ill-luck. He brusquely asked the young man his business, seeing that he made no effort to tell it, and then the young man said he had come to the city and thought he would like to look around the office. Mr. Maxwell rang for a boy, and telling him to show the young man about, shortly dismissed him. In a few days after he received a batch of poetry from the young man, but though of remarkable merit, Mr. Maxwell thought it too sombre in tone for his publication, so he enclosed it with one of the printed slips used for rejected manuscripts. In a day or so Mr. Maxwell was shocked to read of the young man's death. He had gone out to the park, and sitting down on a bench, beside the lake, put a revolver to his ear and so killed himself. He fell off the bench and into the lake, and his body was not found until the next day. He had a letter in his pocket requesting that his body be cremated. He left enough money to pay the expenses, and word for one of his friends that he could do as he wished with his ashes."

"Well, many people do the same thing," Richard said, rather unfeelingly.

"Yes, but this case was particularly sad," Penelope asserted. "The young man was all alone. He hadn't a relative in the world. He had fought his way up and had just completed his law studies, but had not, as yet, succeeded in obtaining any practice. He was in distress and Mr. Maxwell thinks, as I do, that he was so encouraged when his poem was accepted that he came to the city with the purpose of asking employment of the editor, but being greeted so coldly and roughly, I think he could not tell the object of his visit. On his return to Buffalo, as a last hope, he wrote some poetry which was colored with his own despondent feelings, and when they were all returned to him it was the last straw—he went out and shot himself."

"But what else could Mr. Maxwell have done, Penelope," Richard asked, in a business way. He could not accept work, and pay for it, that was not suitable for his periodical. I don't see how he could reproach himself in that case."

"I do and so does he," she replied stoutly. "It wouldn't have taken any more time to be kind to that man than it took to be unkind to him, and when he rejected the poetry, instead of sending back that brutal printed notice he could have had his stenographer write a line, saying the poetry, though meritorious, was not suitable for his journal. That would, at least, have eased the disappointment."

"But editors haven't time for such things, Penelope."

"Then let them take time. I tell you it takes less time to be kind than to be unkind," she maintained, nodding her head positively.

"If they were not short, bores would occupy all their time," he persisted.

"Richard, we will not argue the case," she

said loftily, as a woman always does when she feels she is being worsted. "You can't make me think anything will excuse a man for being brutal and unkind."

Richard had his own opinion on the subject, but he was wise enough to refrain from trying to make Penelope have a similar one.

"I am going away," she said, presently, finding that Dick was not averse to dropping the discussion. "Auntie has accepted an invitation to go to Washington for a few days to visit Mrs. Senator ———, and I am to go along. I rather dread it, but auntie says they won't know as much about the Park mystery there, and I won't be worried with reporters."

"I hope not," replied Dick, beginning already to feel the ghastly emptiness which pervaded the city for him when Penelope was not in it. As long as he knew Penelope was in the city, even if he did not see her, he had a certain happiness of nearness, but when she was away he felt as desolate as Adam must have done before Eve came.

"Penelope, girlie," he said, with a sudden hope, "could we not be engaged while I am working on this case? It would not embarrass you in any way, for we only need tell your aunt, and it would be such help, such encouragement, such happiness, sweet to me. You see it may take months to solve this mystery." Poor Richard thought it would take years. "And if I only knew, darling, that I had your promise, I could do so much. It would help me to conquer the world. Don't be hard-hearted, dear ; don't be cruel to the one who loves you more than anything on earth or in heaven."

"No, no, Dick, you must wait," said Penelope. "Wait until the mystery is solved, it shouldn't take you a great while "—(Richard sighed)—" and then, and then—"

"Then?" repeated Dick, questioningly.

She looked down with sudden embarrassment; he put his arms around her slender waist and drew her close to him. "Then? my love, my soul!"—

"Dearest, come here!" called Penelope's aunt, in that well-bred voice of hers which charmed all hearers, but at this particular moment was very exasperating to Dick. "Richard, come, I want you to see the man standing on the other side of the Avenue. I have been watching him and I think it is quite probable that he is watching the house. Are we never to have done with that Park mystery business?"

They all looked cautiously through the curtains, and they all agreed that the man was watching the house for some purpose.

"They are after you, Dick," exclaimed Penelope. "Oh, I am so afraid this will result seriously to you."

Richard thought so too, only where she

was concerned, though; but he did not give voice to his fears.

" My dear child," laughed the aunt, with that pleasant ring. " Do not talk such nonsense! Richard is able to take care of himself, and especially now that he knows some one is following him."

Shortly afterwards Dick took his leave of Penelope. She maintained an air of cheerfulness as he said farewell, but though the mouth was merry, the sad eyes which met his seemed to whisper the nearness of tears.

Catching up his walking-stick, Richard hastily left the house. He was feeling so blue that he was almost savage. He thought of the man who had been watching the house, and he looked to see if he was still there, half tempted to hunt the fellow out and pull his nose.

Sure enough, the man was there and, as Richard started down the Avenue, he sneaked

along on the other side, much after the manner
of a disobedient dog who had been told to stay
at home.   Dick hailed a passing stage, after
walking a little way, and almost as soon as he
was seated the man also got in.   Richard was
not in a mood to bear watching, so he jumped
out when he saw an empty hansom cab, and,
engaging it, told the driver to cross town.
He did not drive far until he had made sure
that he had eluded his would-be follower, and
having no appetite yet for dinner he ordered
the driver to go to Central Park, where he
paid and dismissed him.

Now that he was alone, he became conscious of a desire to visit the scene of the
mystery which promised to be so fatal to his
happiness.

"I'll go there and think it over," he mused;
"it may give me some idea how to work it
out."   And on he walked over the course he
and Penelope had taken that direful morning.

Night was coming on and the Park was deserted, except for an occasional workman taking a hurried cut across the Park home. How dreary and quiet everything was, and then he thought about the officer who had made himself so obnoxious. This led him to wonder if there were no policemen on duty at night in the Park. He could not remember of ever having noticed any the few times he had visited the Park after nightfall, and there were none visible now anywhere.

He stopped to look for a few moments at the bench where they had found the dead girl, and then he walked on until he came to a bench near the reservoir, where he sat down, and lighting a cigarette gave himself up to unhappy thoughts on his unhappy position.

"If only the Fates would throw something in my way to help me solve that mystery," he thought. "Unless the most extraordinary things occur I shall never be able to tell any-

thing about it. Penelope firmly believes it
was a murder, but I can't see what grounds she
has for it. She thinks it was a deliberate and
well-planned murder, because no one has
claimed the girl, and I sometimes think so myself, but how to prove it?—that's the question."

And Dick gazed seriously at the space of
light made by the opening for the reservoir,
and on to the dense thickness of trees where
night seemed to be lurking, ready to pounce
down on all late comers.

As he looked he became aware of something moving between him and the spot of
light. He was a brave young man, yet his
heart beat a little quicker as he strained his
eyes to see what the moving object was.

Again it passed in view, and this time it
looked to be something climbing; another
moment and it was on the edge of the reservoir.

Now, plainly outlined between him and the strip of light sky, he saw the figure of a woman, a slender girl with flowing hair.

Quick as a flash came the horrible thought that she had come there to die—that she intended to commit suicide.

With a choking cry of horror he ran swiftly towards her.

CHAPTER IV.

STORY OF THE GIRL WHO ATTEMPTED SUICIDE.

Richard Treadwell sat moodily on a bench, half supporting the limp form of the girl he had just saved from death.

He had caught her just as she threw up her hands with a pitiful, weak cry, ready to spring into the reservoir.

"My dear young woman, don't take on so," he said, vexedly, as the girl leaned against his shoulder, and sobbed in a heart-broken, distracted manner. "You are safe now."

As if that could be consolation to a woman who was seeking death which sought her not.

"Really, I am sorry, you know, but there's

a good girl, don't cry," making a ludicrous attempt to console her. "I did it before I thought; if I had known how much you would have been grieved, I—I assure you, upon my honor, I wouldn't have done it. I—I haven't much to live for, either, still when I saw what you intended to do—it shocked me that you should be so desperate. Now that it's all over I wouldn't cry any more. I'd laugh, as if it were a joke, you know. I'd say the fates had saved me for some treat they had reserved for me. There, that's better, don't cry, you are not hurt—not even wet."

The girl broke into a nervous, hysterical laugh, in which the sobs struggled for mastery. Dick, much relieved, added a laugh that sounded rather hollow and mirthless.

"I c-can't help it," said she, haltingly and endeavoring to stop her sobs. "It seems so unreal to be still living when I wanted to be dead. I—I thought it all over, and it seemed

so comforting to think of it being ended.
Then I couldn't see, nor think, nor hear, nor
suffer.   Oh, why did you stop me?"

"I didn't know, you see; I didn't understand it all.   I thought you would regret it—
that you were making a mistake," he tried to
say cheerfully. .

"What right has anybody—what right had
you to prevent me from ending my life?   I
don't want to live!   I am tired of life and of
misery.   I want to know what right any one
has to interfere—to make me live a life that
doesn't concern them and only brings me
misery?" she cried, indignantly.

"Come now, don't be so cast down."   At
this burst of anger Richard was himself again.
"Tell me all about it; maybe I can help you.
Have things gone wrong?"

"Have they ever gone right?   Don't
preach to me.   It's easy to preach to people
who have friends and money and home.

Save your sermons for them. I have nothing! I am all alone in this great big heartless world. I haven't a cent, a home or a friend, and I'm tired of it all. There is no use in talking to me. Some people get it all, and the others get nothing. I am one of the unlucky ones, and the only thing for me to do is to die."

"Why, my good girl, there is surely some·thing better for you than death."

"There is nothing but trouble and hunger, and sometimes work. Do you call that better than death?" she cried despondently.

What a story her few words contained! But Richard, happy, careless, fortunate, little understood their real import.

He knew the girl was very much depressed and morbid, so he concluded it might have a beneficial effect if he could induce her to relate her woes to him.

How mountainous our troubles grow when we brood over them.

How they dwindle into little ant-heaps when we relate them to another.

Richard talked in his frank, healthy way to the girl, and it was not long until she told him the simple, pathetic story of her life.

Her name was Dido Morgan, she said. She was a country girl, the only child of a village doctor, who lived in comfort but died penniless. Her mother died at her birth. She had been raised well, and when reduced to poverty she was too proud to go to work in her native village, so after her father was buried she came to New York.

She soon found that without experience and references she could not get any desirable work in New York. When all other things failed, she, at last, in desperation, applied for and obtained a position in a paper-box factory. She was fortunate enough to learn the work rapidly, and in a few months was able to earn as much as the best workers. She rented a little room on the top floor of a large tenement-house, where she slept and cooked her food. Every week she managed to save a little out of her scant earnings.

One day a girl who worked at the same table with Dido, and who had for a long time been her friend, fainted. The girls crowded around them as Dido knelt on the floor to bathe the sick girl's head and rub her hands.

"Aha! Away from yer tables durin' work hours. I'll pay yer fer this, I'll dock every one of you," yelled the foreman, who at this instant entered the work-room.

The girls, frightened, crept quietly back to their work, but Dido still continued to bathe the girl's head.

" Here, you daisy on the floor, you'll disobey me, hey? I'll dock yer twice," brutally spoke the foreman as he caught a glimpse of Dido's head across the table.

She looked at him with scorn. If glances could kill, he would have died at her feet. Still, she managed to say, quietly:

"Maggie Williams has fainted."

"And because a girl faints must all the shop stop work and disobey rules, eh? I'll pay yer for this. I'll teach yer," he vowed, as he quitted the room.

Dido, unmindful of his brutal threats, turned her attention to Maggie, who in a short time opened her eyes and tried to rise.

"Lie still awhile yet, Maggie," urged her self-appointed nurse. "I'll hold your head on my knee. Don't you feel better now?"

But the girl made no reply. Her small gray eyes stared unblinkingly, unseeingly, up at the smoked rafters of the ceiling.

"What is it, Maggie?" asked the kindly Dido, smoothing the wet, tangled hair, her slender fingers expressing the sympathy which found no utterance in words. "Are you still ill? Shall I take you home to your mother?"

The stare in the small gray eyes grew softer and softer; the corners of the mouth drew down into a pitiful curve, the under lip quivering like a tiny leaf in a strong wind; turning her face down, she sobbed vehemently.

Drawing the poor thin body into a closer embrace, Dido sought to comfort the weeping girl.

Some of the nearest workers hearing those low, heavy sobs, started nervously, and their hands were not as cunning as usual as they covered the boxes, but they dared not go near their unhappy companion or speak the sympathy they felt.

"I'm awfully sorry, Maggie," whispered Dido, "don't cry so; you'll feel better by-and-by."

" Mother's dead," blurted out Maggie.

Dido was stunned into silence by this com-
munication.   She could say nothing.

What could you say to a girl when her
mother is dead?

What could console a girl at such a time?

Maggie told Dido that the dead body of
her mother, who, for a year past, had been
confined to her bed with consumption, was
lying alone, uncared for, at home.

"I loved her so, and I did't want her to
die," she said pitifully.   "I was afraid to go
home after work for fear I'd find her dead, and
I was afraid to sleep at night for fear she'd be
dead when I woke up.   She lay so still, and
she looked so white and death-like, and I
would lean on my elbow and watch her, fearing her breath would stop.   Every few moments I prayed, 'O God, save her!' 'O God,
have mercy!'   I—I couldn't say more, and I
would swallow down the thing that would

choke my throat and wink away the tears that
would come, and watch and watch, until I
couldn't bear the doubt any longer, then I
would touch her gently with my foot to see if
she was still warm, and that would wake her,
and I would be so sorry.

"All last night I never took my eyes off
her dear face," Maggie continued between her
sobs, and Dido was softly crying, too, then.

"She wouldn't eat the things I had brought
her, and when I talked to her she didn't seem
to understand, but said things about father,
who died so long ago, and once or twice she
laughed, but it only made me cry. She didn't
seem to see me either, and when I spoke
to her it only started her to talk about
something else, so I watched and watched. I
didn't pray any more. Somehow all the
prayer had left my soul. Just before morning
she got very still, sometimes a rolling sound
would gurgle in her throat, but when I offered

her a drink she couldn't swallow, and then
I called to her—I couldn't stand it any longer
—'Mother, mother, speak to me. I have always
loved you, speak to me once,' and her dear
lips moved and I bent over her, holding my
breath for fear I would not hear, and she
whispered: 'Lucille—my—pretty—one,' and
then her eyes opened and her head fell to one
side, but she didn't see; she was dead—dead
without one word to me, and I loved her so."

*   *   *   *   *

Dido Morgan shared her own scant dinner
with Maggie that day, and the unhappy girl
remained at work that she might earn some
money, which would help towards burying her
mother.

That afternoon foreman Flint came in,
and, nailing a paper to the elevator shaft, told
the girls to read it, saying he'd teach them to
disobey another time, and that next week they
would work harder for their money.

In fear and trembling the girls crowded timidly about the shaft to read what new misery the foreman had in store for them. They instinctively felt it was a reduction, and the first glance proved their fears were not unfounded.

Some of the girls began to cry, and Dido, the bravest and strongest, spoke excitedly to them of the injustice done them. Even now they were working for less than other factories were paying.

" There is surely justice for girls as well as men somewhere in the world, if we only demand it," she cried, encouragingly. " Let us demand our rights. We will all go down, and I will tell the proprietor that we cannot live under this new reduction. If he promises us the old prices, we will return to work. If he refuses, we will strike."

The braver girls heartily joined the scheme, and the weaker ones naturally fell in, not

knowing what else to do under the circumstances, and frightened at their own boldness.

Dido Morgan, taking little Margaret Williams by the hand, naturally headed the line,
and the girls quietly marched after her, two
by two, down the almost perpendicular stairs.

Dido stopped before the ground-glass door
on the first floor, on which was inscribed:

TOLMAN BIKE,
PRIVATE.

Her heart beat very quickly, but clasping
Maggie's hand closer, she opened the door
and entered.

CHAPTER V.

THE FAILURE OF THE STRIKE.

Tolman Bike was engaged in conversation with foreman Flint when Dido opened the door and entered.

He lifted his head, and never noticing Dido, fixed a look of absolute horror on Maggie Williams's tear-stained and swollen face, as he rose pale and trembling and gasped in a husky tone :

" Why do you come to me ?"

Margaret gazed stupidly at him with her small, grey eyes, offering no reply.

Dido, greatly astonished at Mr. Bike's manner, stammered out that she represented the girls he employed, who had decided to appeal to him not to enforce the proposed reduction, as they were already working for less than other factories were paying.

When she began to speak a strange look of relief passed over his face and with a peculiar, nervous laugh, he sat down again.

"Get out of this," said he roughly. "If you don't like my prices leave them for those who do."

Turning his back to the girls he coolly began arranging the papers on his desk.

When Dido began to plead for justice he calmly ordered foreman Flint to "remove these young persons."

"If you do dare touch me, I'll kill you!" exclaimed Dido in a rage, as Flint made a movement to obey orders.

He cowered, stepped back and stammered an excuse to his employer. He felt the scorch in Dido's blazing midnight eyes and he respected her warning and his own person.

Mr. Bike moved quietly to the door and holding it open, said :

" My beauty, you be careful, or that fine spirit of yours will get you into trouble some of these days."

Dido gave him a scornful glance as she and Maggie walked out, and the door was closed behind them.

She related her failure to the waiting girls, and they all went home after promising to be there Monday morning to prevent others taking their places. They seemed to feel the consequence of their own act less than Dido and rather welcomed an extra holiday.

That evening Dido pawned all her furniture and extra clothes, and the money she received for them, added to her savings, went towards saving the body of Mrs. Williams from the Potter's Field. There was not quite enough to pay the undertaker, so Dido was forced to borrow the remainder from Blind

Gilbert, the beggar, who occupied the room in the rear of that occupied by the Williamses.

Monday morning the girls all gathered around the entrance to the factory and urged the new girls, who came in answer to an advertisement, not to apply for work and thereby injure their chances of making the strike successful.

Only the foreigners stubbornly refused the girls' request, and they applied for and received the work which the others had abandoned. Tuesday more foreigners were given work, and the weaker strikers, getting frightened at this, quitted their companions and returned to the factory.

This so enraged the other strikers that they waited for the deserters in the evening, when they were going home from work. They first tried to persuade their weaker companions to reconsider their decision and somehow the argument ended in a fight.

Dido Morgan, who was stationed as a picket further down the street, came rushing up to the struggling, pulling, crying girls, hoping to pacify them.

Almost instantly foreman Flint arrived, accompanied by an officer. Pointing out Dido, with a diabolical grin he told the officer to arrest her. The now frightened girls fell back while the officer dragged Dido away, despite her protests.

That night she spent in the station-house, and in the morning she was taken to the Essex Market Court, where the Judge, listening to the policeman's highly imaginative story, asked her what she had to say, and though she endeavored to tell the truth, hustled her off with "ten days or ten dollars."

Being penniless she was sent to the Island, where she spent the most miserable ten days of her life.

But her final release brought her no happiness or joy. She knew that it was useless to return to her bare rooms, because of the rent being overdue, and she had no friend but Margaret Williams, who had as much as she could manage to provide for herself.

Disheartened, penniless and hungry, she spent the day wandering around from one place to another, begging for any kind of work. At every place they complained of having more workers than they needed.

Night came on and she thought of the Christian homes, ostensibly asylums for such unfortunate beings as herself. She applied to several along Second Avenue and Bleecker Street, but she found no refuge in any. They were either filled, or because she had no professed religion and had long since quit attending church, they barricaded their Christian (?) quarters against her.

The last and only place, in which they

made no inquiries about religion, they charged twenty cents for a bed, and so the weary, hungry girl was forced again to go out into the darkness.

She noticed an open door, leading to a dispensary, on Fourth Avenue, and hiding herself in a dark corner of the hallway there, she spent the night,

In the morning she got a glass of milk and a cup of broth in the diet kitchen, and then she resumed her search for work.

It was useless. Tired out and discouraged she wandered on and on, until she came to the Park. The unhappy girl sought the enticing shade, where she watched the gay, merry people who passed before her. The more she saw, the more despondent she became. They looked so blest, so happy.

Life gave them everything and gave her nothing.

It began to grow dark, and every one hurried from the Park. She had no place to go, no one to care for her, nothing to live for, and she walked further into the Park, helpless, hopeless.

How grand it would be to rest for evermore!

The thought came and charmed her. How sweet, how blessed a long, easy, senseless slumber would be with no pain, no unhappiness, no hunger!

She noticed the reservoir, she climbed up and looked in. Like a bed of velvet the dark waters lay quietly before her, and the rough darkness of the surrounding country seemed to warn her to partake of what was within her reach.

A great wave of peace welled up in her heart, her weariness disappeared in an exquisite languor, which enwrapped her body and mind.

"'Rest, everlasting rest,' rang soothingly

in my ears," said Dido, in conclusion, "and with a little cry of joy I went to plunge in "——

" And I saved you from a very rash deed," broke in Dick. " My poor girl, don't you know there are hundreds of noble-hearted people in New York who are always ready to help the unfortunate ? There is charity and Christianity in some places."

" But they are hard to find," said the girl, " and they do not exist in so-called benevolent homes."

" Now, I tell you what we will do," said Dick, cordially, lighting a match and looking at his watch. " We will first try to find some-thing to eat, for I am beastly hungry, and then I will take you to your friend, Maggie Wil-liams, if you will kindly show the way, and we will see what can be done for a young woman who gives up so easily."

To be frank, Richard doubted the girl's

story. Yet he did not want to act hastily in the matter. If the girl had suffered all she said, he felt that not only would he gladly help her, but Penelope would be delighted to make life brighter for the poor victim of fate. So he decided to take her to the home of Margaret Williams, if such a person really existed, and learn from others the true story, if what she had told him should prove to be false.

In this Richard showed himself very wise for a young man. If it was really a case of charity no one would be kinder or more liberal, but he doubted.

CHAPTER VI.

IS THE GIRL HONEST?

In a small oyster-house near the Park they found something to eat, and Dick also found that he had saved the life of a remarkably pretty girl.

At any other time Dick Treadwell would have scorned to eat dinner—and such a dinner —at such a place. This night he not only ate, but enjoyed it. He never noticed the uninviting appearance of the big, fat German waiter who had, when they first came in, leaned with both hands on the table and said briefly, and with a rising accent, " Beer ?"

He slapped his dirty towel over the sticky

circular spots on the table as Richard ordered
dinner from a card that looked as if it had
never served any other purpose than that of
fly-paper.

The waiter went out, after receiving the
order, carefully closing the door after him.
The room was evidently meant for small
parties, for the only thing in it was the table
and four chairs.

" Don't you think the room is too warm ?"
Dick asked, and hardly waiting for his guest's
reply, he got up and opened wide the door.

The waiter spread a cotton napkin over the
table before Dick and Dido Morgan, and set
some pickles and crackers, and pepper and salt,
and two little bits of butter, the size and
shape of a half dollar, on the table; then he
brought the clams.

This done he went out again, very carefully closing the door after him. Richard
called to him, but he did not answer, so Dick

got up and opened the door himself. Dido
Morgan looked at him with an innocent, ques-
tioning smile. She had no idea that Dick
could possibly have any other reason for opening the door, than that it made the room
cooler. When the waiter come in the next
time he closed the door. Richard's face
flushed angrily as he said sternly :

" I wish that door open. You will please
leave it so."

The waiter gave an impudent, almost familiar grin, but the door was open during the rest
of the dinner.

As Dido Morgan sat opposite Dick eating
daintily but appreciatively, the color came into
her dark, creamy cheeks, and her brown eyes
sparkled like the reflection of the sun in a
still, dark pool. Her loose, damp hair, hanging in little rings about her broad brow and
white throat, was very appealing to the artistic
sense.

And her look—it was so frank, so sincere, so trusting, and her eyes had such a way of looking startled, that Dick felt a warmer thrill of interest invade his soul than he ever thought possible for any other girl than Penelope.

Before dinner was finished Richard had called her " Miss Dido," and " Dido," and she had not even thought of resenting it.

There are a great many false ideas that are forgotten in such moments as these.

The one had seen the other face death, and a human feeling had for the time swept all false pretenses and hollow etiquette away.

They drove down to Mulberry Street in a coupé, and if such a thing was unusual to the young girl whom Richard rescued, it was well hidden under a manner of ease that suggested familiarity.

" There is where Maggie Williams lived," she said, as they turned down Mulberry Street.

Richard leaned forward, but in the semi-light got little idea of the appearance of the place.

"She may have gone from there by this time," Dido continued, showing a slight hesitation that threatened to shake Dick's not over-strong confidence in her. "She lived there when I went away, but so many things happen in such short time among the poor."

"Don't stop the driver," she said, quickly, as Dick pounded on the glass with the head of his walking-stick. "Drive on to the corner. It is such an unusual sight to see a carriage stop before these houses, that it would likely attract a crowd, and you don't want to do that ?"

"Why ?" asked Dick, curiously. When he could not see her face he liked her less.

"Well, you look so unlike the people who live in this neighborhood, and if you attract notice, you might find it a very uncomfortable place for an elegant young man to be in at almost midnight," Dido Morgan said, with a light laugh ; then, taking matters into her own hands, she opened the door of the coupé, and called the driver to stop.

Richard had no sooner dismissed the driver than he regretted it. He again felt the old mistrust of the strange girl, and recollections of tales he had read of female trappers and the original snares they lay for their victims returned forcibly to his mind.

He felt he was a fool to come here at night, but he was ashamed to go back now. The night was warm and the heat had driven many of the people out of the tenements in search of a breath of air, and the dark groups of silent men and women who filled the door-steps and basement entrances and curbstones, and the ill-favored people who passed them offered Dick little hope for succor, if indeed he was the victim of a plot.

There were no policemen to be seen any-

where, although Dick knew the police headquarters were not far distant.

Quietly he walked beside the girl, who, too,
had grown silent. He scorned to confess his
fears, and he felt a determination to meet
what there might be waiting for him, even if it
be death, before he would weaken and retreat.

The girl entered the doorway of a dark,
dilapidated house, the only doorway which
had no lounger, a fact in itself suspicious to
Dick. He, with many misgivings and a
decided palpitation of the heart, stumbled on
the step as he started to follow.

Had he done right and was he safe in
trusting and following this clever girl?

Before he had time to decide she caught
his hand and led him into the dark hall.

A little weak thought, that doubtless holding his hand was part of the plan to give him
less chance for self-defense, flashed through
his mind.

Gropingly he put forth his other hand, and a thrill of horror shot through him like an electric shock as it came in contact with a man's coat and a warm, yielding body.

CHAPTER VII.

MR. MARTIN SHANKS : GUARDIAN.

"Did you run against something?" asked Dido, as she felt Richard start.

"It's only me," said a deep bass voice, which had such an honest and harmless ring, that Richard's fear and nervousness dropped from him like a cloak.

"It's all right," Dido responded cheerfully, as she stopped and knocked on a door.

Dick knew it was a door from the sound, but he was unable to distinguish door from wall in the darkness.

It was opened by some one inside. Dick

saw the outlines of a girlish figure between himself and the light, and heard a surprised exclamation : " Why, Dido !"

They stepped in, and the girl closed the door and hastened to set chairs for her visitors.

" Mr. Treadwell, this is Margaret Williams," said Dido ; then turning to Maggie she added, simply, " Mr. Treadwell has been kind to me."

" We were frightened about you," Maggie said, her eyes beaming warmly on Dido. " I heard you got in trouble 'round at the shop. I went out to look you up, but I couldn't find out anything about you either at the station-house or at your house."

"I s'pose you know," she added, " that the girls went in ? Yes, the strike is off. They wouldn't take me back, so I'm doing what I can for Blind Gilbert, and he pays rent and buys what we eat."

Dido, in a few simple words, frankly told Maggie all that had befallen her since her arrest. She did not omit her rash attempt to commit suicide, and Richard's timely intervention.

Meanwhile Richard had taken a glance about the little bare room.

A plain, single-board table, covered with a bit of badly worn oilcloth, had been pulled out into the room, and they now sat around it. A little low oil lamp, with a broken chimney —which had been patched with a scrap of paper—was the only light in the room. Dick carefully slipped a paper bill under the newspaper which lay on the table where Margaret had flung it when she came to open the door for them.

A small stove stood close to the wall, and on it was a tin coffee-pot and an iron tea-kettle with a broken spout.

Above the stove was a little shelf, which

held some tallow candles in a jar, and some upturned flat-irons.

The bed looked very unsafe and uncomfortable. It was covered with a gayly colored calico patchwork quilt. The patchwork was made in some set pattern, which was unlike anything Richard had ever seen or dreamed of.

Several pieces of as many carpets lay on the floor, and a much worn blanket was hung on two nails over the window, to take the place of a shade or curtain.

Dick's heart ached at the evident signs of poverty, and a warm instinct of protection possessed him.

"I hope you will allow me to be of some assistance to you," he said, when the girls, having finished their confessions, became silent. "I think I can, in a few days, assure Miss Dido of a better position than the one she has lost."

As he spoke, there came a timid knock on the door, and Maggie sprang to open it.

" I jest thought I'd drop in tew see how you wuz gettin' along, Maggie," said from the darkness the same deep bass voice that had restored Richard's courage in the hall-way.

It was followed by a tall, lank man, who awkwardly held a black, soft felt hat in his big red hands. His rough clothes seemed to hang on him, and he held one shoulder higher than the other in an apologetic manner, as if to assure the world that his towering above the average height of people was neither his fault nor desire. His bushy and unattrac-tive dust-colored hair seemed determined to maintain the stiffness which its owner lacked. His red mustache and chin-whiskers were resolved to out-bristle his hair. His shaggy eyebrows overhung modest blue eyes that looked at if they fain would draw beneath

those brows as a turtle draws its head under
its shell.

He bashfully greeted Dido, and she
introduced him to Richard as " Mr. Martin
Shanks, who boards with some friends upstairs." He held out his big hand to Dick,
saying :

"Glad to make yer acquaintance, sir !" all
the while blushing vividly.

"We ran against you in the hall, I think,"
ventured Dido.

"Yes, I was standin' there when you came,"
he answered, slowly, shooting a glance from
under his brows at Maggie.

Maggie looked down, and Dido was surprised to see her blush. She would have
been more surprised if Maggie had told her
that this great, big, hulking man had stood
guard at her door every night since her mother
died.

"I should jedge you don't belong to this

yer neighborhood," he remarked to Richard, shooting forth a jealous look.

"You are correct," replied Richard, pleasantly.

"What might yer business be?" he demanded further, nervously turning his hat.

"Down here, or my professional employment?" asked Richard, waking up.

"What do ye do fer a livin?"

"Oh! I see. I'm a lawyer," Dick replied, glibly.

"A lawyer, eh? An' I take it as yer not a married man, else ye wouldn't be payin' attentions to this 'ere orphan girl."

"You don't understand," Maggie interrupted, startled. "Dido was in trouble and Mr. Treadwell found her and brought her here."

"Martin should mind his own business," exclaimed Dido, indignantly. "If this was my house I would show him the door.

"Not on my account," interposed Dick, warmly. "If Mr. Shanks is a friend of the family he has a right to know the reason of a stranger being here."

"These young girls 'ere, sir," explained frightened Martin Shanks, "have no parints to take care on them, an' I says to meself, when Mis' Williams wuz a lyin' dead here, that I'd see no harm come aninst them while I wuz about."

"That was very good of you, Mr. Shanks," cordially replied Dick, and then, bidding the girls good night, he left. Martin Shanks, wishing to see the stranger well out of the neighborhood before he quit his post of guardianship for the remainder of the night, accompanied Dick as far as Broadway, and Dick was not sorry to have his escort.

CHAPTER VIII.

THE MISSING STENOGRAPHER.

When next Richard went to Mulberry
Street, it was to notify Dido Morgan of a
position he had secured for her with a prominent photographer.   Her duties would be
light and not unpleasant, as she was merely
required to take charge of the reception room.

Dido was delighted ; nothing could have
suited her better.   Before her father died, she
had devoted a great deal of time and study to
sketching, and now this work seemed as
though it might lead her nearer to her old
life.

While Richard was talking to the girls he
heard a scraping noise in the hall, and pres-

ently the door opened, and an old man, with
such a decided roundness of the shoulders that
it was almost a hump, felt with his cane the
way before him and apparently finding everything all right entered and closed the door.
A little, short-tailed, spotted dog, with a world
of affection bound up in his black-and-white
hide, slid in beside the man's uncertain legs,
and now stood wiggling his body with a
wiggle that bespoke affection for the man.

"Maggie, is you ready for me and Fritz?"
he asked, timidly,

"Yes, Gilbert," she replied, gently, and she
went to him and guided his uncertain feet to a
chair which stood before the table.

"The young gentleman who was so good
to Dido is here," she explained, and he lifted
his head quickly as if he would like to see.
At this, Richard very thoughtfully came forward and taking the old man's shaking hand,
gave it a warm pressure.

"I'm glad to know you, sir," Blind Gilbert said, deferentially. "May be you know me, sir. It's sixteen years this coming August since I've had a stand on Broadway. I don't do much business, but I'm thankful for all I have. The Lord, in all this mercy, seen fit to afflict me, but he never let old Gilbert starve."

"How did you lose your sight?" Richard asked awkardly, not wishing to express any opinion concerning the mercy of making a man blind.

"Well, it came very sudden like. I had a little shop in this very room, sir, and I lived in the one back, where I've lived ever since I lost my shop. I done a good business, as I had done ever since me and me old woman came out from Ireland, these forty years ago. Me old woman fell sick and after running up a long doctor bill, she died, the Lord bless her soul, for if we had our fights, she was a good woman to me. One mornin' after she had been

put in her grave, I started out to go across
Mulberry Street. The sun was shinin' bright
when I started out the door and it was as fine
a mornin' as I ever seen. When I got to the
middle of the street, everything got as dark as
night and I yelled for help. They took me to
the doctor's but he said I had gone blind and
nothing could help me. Then they took me
to a hospital, and after a while I could see
some light with one eye, but then it left and
they said nothing could be done. I couldn't
stay shut up, so I came back. Me little shop
was gone and everything I owned, so I got a
license and went on to Broadway and begged
until I got enough to rent the back room
again and there I've lived ever since."

"Does what you get pay all your expenses?" Richard asked.

"The city gives me forty dollars a year, and
I manage to makeenough with that to keep me."

Maggie took a newspaper off the table

which disclosed beneath it the table spread for a simple meal. She took a bit of fried steak and some fried potatoes from the oven and set them before Gilbert.

Richard felt somewhat embarrassed and started to leave, but they all urged him so warmly to stay that he sat down again. When Maggie poured out Gilbert's coffee, she offered a cup of it to Dick. He, fearing to hurt her feelings by refusing to partake of what she had made, accepted the great thick cup. It was the worst dose Dick ever took. He tried to maintain an air of enjoyment, but he found it impossible to prevent his face drawing very stiff and grave when he tried to swallow the horrible stuff.

"Won't you have some more coffee? This is warmer," Maggie asked, as Dick at last set the cup down.

"No, no," he answered, thickly, but most decidedly.

Maggie gave him a startled, inquiring look, and poor Richard felt himself blush as he endeavored to swallow the mouthful of coffee-grains he got with the last of the coffee. Finding this unpleasant as well as impracticable, he disposed of them as best he could in his handkerchief and hastened to reassure her.

"I never, never drink coffee until after dinner," he said, earnestly, "and only broke my usual rule on this occasion because you made it."

He gave her a smile with this pretty speech ; while it was not exactly what his pleased smiles usually were, it made Maggie blush with pleasure.

The spotted dog, having swallowed his food after the manner of people at railway stations, came rubbing and sniffling around Richard's knee in a very friendly spirit.

"Fine dog, sir, Fritz is," blind Gilbert said, hearing the dog's sounds. "Gettin' old, though, like the old man. Now, Mag', child, —she's me 'dopted daughter, sir, I never had no children of me own—if you're ready, me girl, we'll start for me place of business."

Maggie put on her hat and fastened a chain to Fritz's collar, and then giving Richard a little smile, took blind Gilbert by the hand and led him out.

" Maggie is very wretched about her sister Lucille," said Dido, confidentially, when left alone with Dick. " She went away two weeks before Mrs. Williams died, and she hasn't come back yet."

" Did she say that she would be away for any time?" Richard asked, with a show of interest that he was far from feeling. He was rather weary of troublesome girls just then.

"No, that's it," eagerly. "They hadn't any idea that she wasn't coming home."

"Indeed! Where had she gone?"

"They don't even know that. She said she was going out to do some extra work."

"What kind of work?"

"She was a typewriter and a stenographer," Dido explained, "and in the evenings she used to get extra work. This night she went to work, but she did not come back, and Maggie worries over it."

"I should think she would," Richard replied kindly. "Why didn't Maggie go to her sister's employer? Probably he could throw some light on the subject."

"She did go to him, and he said Lucille had asked for two weeks' vacation, which he had given her, and Maggie didn't want to tell him that Lucille had gone out to do some extra work, for fear he wouldn't like it. He paid her by the week, and didn't know she did outside work. Maggie thought then she would be back, but now it is five weeks and she hasn't come back yet."

"And poor mother loved her so," added Maggie huskily, as she re-entered the room, having left Blind Gilbert on his corner.

"Do you think we could do anything towards finding her?" Dido asked eagerly.

"I hardly see what you could do, unless you notify the police and advertise for her," Dick replied, listlessly. He had enough girls on his mind now, with Penelope, the Park Mystery girl and Dido, and he did not feel anxious to add another to his already too large list. He felt satisfied to look after Penelope, and was desirous of assuming sole charge of her, but did not want any more.

"I should say that she had received a better position somewhere, and that you will hear from her before long," Dick added, encouragingly.

"Oh, she would surely send for her clothes if she had," Dido said, earnestly. "If you will tell us what to do—what is the best thing—we will try to do it; Maggie is so anxious to find her."

"I can easily do for you all that can be done," Dick replied. "If you can give me a description of her, I will send it to Police Headquarters and have them search for her."

"She was slender, and had a lovely white complexion and blue eyes, and black hair," Dido began, Richard writing it in a little note-book.

"Was she tall or short?" he asked, pausing for a reply.

"About my height—don't you think so, Maggie? I'm five feet four and one-half inches."

"How was she dressed?'

"She had on her black alpaca dress, and wore a round black turban, with a bunch of green grass on the back of it," said Dido.

"And she carried her light jacket along to wear home, 'cause mother thought it would be cold," Maggie said, helping Dido along. "Lucille always had nicer dresses than I had. She was twenty-one, though she didn't look it. I am older than she is."

CHAPTER IX.

THE STRANGER AT THE BAR.

Richard Treadwell sent a description of Maggie Williams' missing sister to the police authorities, and also inserted a cautious but alluring personal in all the leading newspapers; still the missing Lucille did not return, and nothing was heard of her.

"My God, what it is to be poor!" Richard mused one morning as he walked up Broadway. "Why, the glimpses I get during my visits to Mulberry Street, of the trials and privations the poor endure, makes me heartsick. There's Gilbert, blind and helpless, forced to spend his time on a Broadway corner begging his living. Sitting there waiting

for people to give him pennies, and yet he
doesn't want to die. Why, he clings to life as
if he had the wealth of Monte Cristo. And
all those untidy, unhappy women down there,
with peevish, crying, dirty children, live on in
their garrets and cellars, for what ?

" They have no pleasures, no happiness,
no comfort, and they are raising families to
live out the same miserable existence. Ugh !

"And there are Maggie and Dido ! They
live in that miserable, God-forsaken room, and
haven't a decent-looking dress to their backs.
There are no drives, no jewels, no pretty
dresses, no fond petting for them, yet, bless
their brave hearts, they are more cheerful than
most girls I know who live on the Avenue.
Dido is happy now that she has work, and
Maggie would be happy if it wasn't for her
absent sister. By Jove, I respect those girls.
I admire their spirit, and if I don't find
Maggie's sister it won't be my fault. It's just

as easy to solve the mystery of two girls, as it is to solve the mystery of one," he thought, with grim humor, as he had made no progress in either case.

"I haven't the least doubt that Maggie's sister, tiring of the poverty at home, found snugger quarters and is sticking to them. If I only knew what she looked like I would likely run across her in some of my rounds. New York is a very little place to those that go about. I'll wager if I knew that girl, and she was running around, I'd meet her inside of three evenings. If I could only identify her—— By Jove! I have it. I'll get Dido, who knows the girl, and I'll take her to the places where we are likely to meet the missing sister. Whew! Why didn't I think of it before? If I don't know all about her inside of a week I'll think—well, I'll find the little scamp, that's all."

Delighted with his new scheme, Richard

cut across Twenty-fourth Street and went into
the Hoffman House bar-room.   Without stop-
ping he went through to the office, where he
wrote and sent a note to Dido, asking her to
take dinner with him that evening.   Then he
walked back to the bar to congratulate himself—after the manner of his sex—for taking the road, whose way, he thought, led to
success.

Richard stood before the famous bar and
marvelled how daylight seemed to rob the
room of half its fascination.   The men of the
world, the men of fashion, the outlandish
youth of dudedom, the be-diamonded actor
and bejewelled men whose modes of life
would ill bear investigation, had all fled with
the night.

The Flemish tapestry looked dull, and the
exquisite Eve was a less glaring white, and
seemed to have lost expression in a new-
found modesty, and the nymphs and satyr

looked dull and tired. How different from the hours when the gas brought beautiful colors into the cut-glass pendants on the chandeliers, and everything seemed awake and alive where now they slept. The bartenders looked dull and uninterested, and a man who stood alone at the bar drank as if he had nothing else to do.

He was a low, heavy-set man, dressed handsomely. He wore a black beard and mustache, and his small, black, bright eyes critically surveyed, across his high nose, the handsome and genial Richard. He set down an empty whiskey glass from which he had just been drinking, and, after taking a swallow of ice water, he remarked, in a voice perfectly void of emotion:

"I beg your pardon, but do you know that you are being 'shadowed'?"

"I knew they were after me some days ago, but I thought they had given me up,"

Dick said, laughingly. "What do you know about it ?"

"I saw a man dog after you to the office when you first went through, and when you returned he came after you and went on out the side door. He'll be on the watch for you when you go out," he continued, in that even, passionless voice.

"You are very kind," Dick said, gratefully, "to warn me of the fellow."

"The game was too easy, if you didn't know," he said, with a malicious grin. "I only wanted to give the fellow some work—make him earn his money. You can both work at the same game now."

"You are very kind," Dick repeated, mechanically. He had a faint impression that the stranger had warned him of his followers more with malicious motives than with any feeling of good will, still the next moment he felt ashamed of harboring such a thought against the man.

"If you care to know the fellow, I'll walk out with you and point him out," the man offered gruffly, still with a gleam in his eyes which showed that the expected discomfort of the two men afforded him if not exactly pleasure, at least, amusement.

"Thank you. Won't you join me first?" asked Dick. "What will you have? Whiskey"—to the bartender. "I am very much obliged for your kindness, and if I can ever be of any service to you, command me," and the impulsive Dick took his card case from his pocket and handed one of the rectangular bits of pasteboard to the man just as they both lifted their glasses.

The stranger glanced at the name and turned ghastly pale. His glass fell from his nerveless fingers to the floor with a crash, and he leaned heavily against the mahogany bar.

CHAPTER X.

TOLMAN BIKE.

One evening Mr. Richard Treadwell found the following letter awaiting him when he went to his rooms to dress for dinner.

"Washington, *June Third*, 18—.
" Dear Dick :
"I am glad to say our prolonged visit has drawn to a close, and to-morrow we return to dear old New York and—Dick. I wonder how much we have been missed. You cannot imagine how anxious I am to see you. I feel sure that you are ready to tell me all about the poor dead girl.

"You can't imagine how I feel about her. Auntie says I am morbid and depressed. When I go to bed at night and close my eyes I can see her again lying before us, her masses of golden hair, her pretty little hands, her delicate clothes, and I can't go to sleep for wondering whose darling she was and how she came to stray so far away from home and that they never found her.

"I firmly believe she eloped with some rascal who tired of her at last and murdered her to free himself.

"When will you solve this unhappy mystery?

"Your short, unsatisfactory letters, I have felt all along, were a mere blind to keep me from suspecting the surprising story you have in reserve for me.

"If you have been wasting your time in being devoted to some of the many girls who used to attract your attention, and neglecting the Park mystery case, I feel that I can never forgive you.

"I forgot to tell you in my last that we met Clara Chamberlain and her mother here. They came over for a day to arrange with their lawyers something about Clara's Washington property. Clara confessed to me that the report which was published awhile ago concerning her engagement was true. You remember none of us credited it at the time. Well, it is true, and the wedding is to be celebrated privately on the seventh. Auntie is to go and I promised Clara I would be there. Will this not be rather a blow to your friend Chauncey Osborne?

"Her fiancé, I believe, is quite unknown in our set. You know how very peculiar dear Clara always was! She, of course, says that he is charming and a man of culture and ability, a prominent politician and bound to make a stir in the world.

"Auntie met an old friend here, Mr. Schuyler, who went to school with auntie. They have been living their school-days over again—it seems they were boy and girl lovers —and to hear them laugh over the things they used to do makes me laugh from very sympathy.

"Do you know, girls don't have half the fun now that they did in auntie's day. I will never be able, when I get to be an old woman, to sit down and recall with a playmate the funny scrapes we got into when we were children. When I hear auntie and Mr. Schuyler talk, I feel so sorry that my life has been so common-place.

"But there—I have written four times as much as you did in your last. Mr. Schuyler is going over to New York with us, and we are going to show him about. He has not been there since he was a boy.

" Hoping you have been a good boy during my absence, I am,

"Very sincerely your (s),

" PENELOPE."

To

'RICHARD TREADWELL, Esqre.,

" ' The Washington,'

" New York City."

"I forgot to say that Clara's fianceé, I
have been told, is the sole proprietor of some
kind of a factory downtown which assures him
quite a nice income. His name is Tolman
Bike. Did you ever hear of him?"

"The name sounds familiar to me,"
thought Dick, as he folded the letter and put
it in his pocket. "Still I do not remember
ever knowing such a person. Probably I re-
collect it, from reading that notice of Clara's
engagement, although I had forgotten the whole
matter."

Dick Treadwell was not feeling very easy. He longed for Penelope's return, yet he dreaded it, knowing that he had no progress to report in the task she had imposed upon him. He had thought she would be pleased with his conduct in regard to Dido Morgan and Maggie Williams, but when she had expressed a hope that he had not been devoting himself to girls and wasting the time that belonged to the work he had undertaken, he felt a little dubious as to the way in which she would receive any account of the part he took with the poor girls whom he wished to befriend.

Isn't the matter of likes and dislikes a strange thing?" Dick asked, when, an hour later, he and Dido Morgan were dining together. He refilled the glasses which stood by their plates. "This is very good wine, don't you think? Let me help you to some spaghetti. I have often wondered why at first meeting we conceive a regard for some people and a dislike for others.

"You remember the incident I related to you the first, or rather the second time you dined with me, of the man I met in the Hoffman House who warned me that I was shadowed. Well, I have run across him several times since. I have the strangest feeling for him, and he apparently dislikes me. I can't say that I like him, but I have such a desire to be with and near him that I can't say I dislike him either. By Jove, I was surprised when he fell against the bar that day and looked so miserably ill. I thought at first it was the sight of my name that affected him, but he assured me that it was a spasm of the heart, a chronic complaint of his."

"What was his name?" asked Dido, breaking off a bit of bread. She was growing prettier every day since Richard had secured a

position for her, and to-night she was bewitch-
ing in a new gray cloth gown.

"Clark, he said ; I think I asked him for
it," said Dick, laughing.

"You don't seem to have tired of going
around to all sorts of restaurants," he continued, noticing the happy expression on Dido's
pretty face.

"Tired of it !"

Her tone but faintly expressed what
untold happiness those evenings had been to
her.

"I thought you would be disgusted with
our search before it was half finished," he said,
looking admiringly into her soft brown eyes
that had given him one of those startled
glances which half bewitched him.

"It has been heaven !" she said, with a
sigh of rapture. "I love the bright lights,
and the well-dressed, happy people, and the
busy, silent waiters, and the white linen and

the fine dishes. Oh, I think people who can take their dinners out all the time must be very, very happy."

"You would not think so if you were a poor, forlorn man," he said, smiling at her enthusiasm, "and had to dine out three hundred and sixty-five times a year, not counting breakfast and luncheon. I've started out evenings and I've stopped on Broadway and wondered where on earth I should eat. Delmonico's, St. James, Hoffman, all are old stories, clear down the list. Here I had luncheon, there probably I had breakfast, the other place I dined last night or the night before, and at last I turn down some cross street, and go into a cheap place where a fellow can't get a mouthful that it doesn't gag him, so I'll have an appetite to-morrow. I hate the sight of a bill of fare and I get so that I'll fool around for half an hour until some man near me orders, and then I order the same thing. I tell you its dreadful not to know where to eat."

" I suppose that is the reason some men marry ?" she asked, brightly.

"Well, not exactly," he said, flushing slightly.

" Do the people you see in the restaurants never interest you ?" Dido asked, seeing he had become silent.

"No, I never notice them unless it is some one with loud dress or manners, and then I watch them as I watch a lot of monkeys in a cage."

" Every place I go I see some one interesting," Dido said, slowly. "Look at that fat woman over there, in the cherry-red dress and hat. See how proud that little dark man looks of having such a woman with him. I have heard her tell him of her former great triumphs as an actress, and I can imagine a story of her life. See that slender, pretty, dark-eyed girl, with very white brow, and very red cheeks, and very dark shadows about her eyes, and very, very golden hair. See her smile and talk to that insipid-looking man, with an enormous nose and bald head and eye-glasses, whose 'villain's mustache,' carries a sample of everything he had for dinner. Now can't you picture that pretty girl is some ballet girl ambitious to rise. He, a man of means and influence, and she forgets his looks and that he talks through his nose, and tries to impress him with her ability."

"Hum !" said Richard, giving Dido a strange smile. "I'm afraid my imagination is not as great or as charitable as yours. Tell me what you think of the party to our left."

"That poor little man without legs ?" asked Dido, quick tears coming to her eyes. "He has a bright, happy face though, and he has diamonds—many of them, on his fingers.

I think that large woman who sits beside him and looks into his eyes so affectionately, loves him very much because of his affliction. I'm sure I would. And that man and woman opposite, though I don't like their looks, seem to heed every word he says and to be very fond of him."

Richard laughed softly.

"Well, Dido, I don't want to spoil your dream, but that little man has a brain that is far out of proportion to his weak and dwarfed body. He stands at the head of his profession, and has accumulated wealth by his industry and ability. Quite a reproach to us worthless fellows, who were born with legs. I have a great admiration for him, but those people with him neither care for him for his ability or his affliction. They are not of that kind."

"What then?" asked Dido, in distress.

"Money—money, child. It's the story you could read at almost every table here.

That's why I don't allow my imagination any liberty in restaurants. Your eyes have not yet tried the worldly glasses which experience has put on mine. And now, while we drink our coffee, let us talk about Maggie's sister."

A girl came through, trying to sell some badly assorted flowers, and a black and yellow bird in a cage, high above their heads, thrusts his long beak and head through the wires and, impudently twisting his head to see what was taking place below him, gave vent at intervals to a shrill, defiant cry.

Meanwhile, Richard lighted a cigarette and resumed the conversation.

" I think it is useless to hunt for Maggie's sister any longer. We have made a pretty thorough search of the resorts where I thought we were likely to meet her. I confess I am disappointed. I was sure we would run across her somewhere, and that you would recognize

her.   Do you think it is possible for you not
to recognize her ?"

" No, indeed !   I'd recognize Lucille Williams anywhere," Dido replied, earnestly.

" My private opinion—don't tell Maggie—
is, that she tired of her family and home and
that she took herself to better quarters and
means to keep them in ignorance of her whereabouts, fearing they would ask her to give
towards their support."

" I hardly think Lucille was as heartless as
that," thoughtfully replied Dido.   "She was
vain and fond of dressing, but I don't think
she would be as mean as that."

" What were her habits ?" asked Dick.

" Habits ?   What she did regularly ?
Well, she used to go to Coney Island and
Rockaway and such places in the Summer, with
some boys she met in the places she worked,
but after she got work in the office at the factory where we worked, she got very steady

and she wouldn't go out with anybody any more. The nights she went out she went to do extra work."

"How did she get along with your employer? You gave me the impression that he was very brutal," Dick said, musingly.

"Oh, Lucille got along splendidly with him. I always thought he was horrible, but she never said anything about him. She was very easy-natured, anyway, and I have a bad temper," said Dido, in a shamefaced way.

" How did he like her, do you know ?"

"Who? Tolman Bike ?" asked Dido, quickly.

"Tolman Bike? Why" — stammered Dick.

" He was the proprietor, you know, and Lucille was his stenographer," exclaimed Dido. " I don't know what he thought of her, for Lucille didn't talk much ; but she seemed to get along well enough."

Dido became silent, as Richard was intent on his own thoughts.

Tolman Bike was the name of the man who was to marry Clara Chamberlain.

Tolman Bike was also the name of the employer of Lucille and Maggie Williams and Dido Morgan.

Tolman Bike, Miss Chamberlain's fianceé, was the proprietor of a down-town factory, so it must be one and the same man.

Well, and if so, could it be possible that Tolman Bike, the man who was engaged to marry a banker's daughter, could have been in love with Lucille Williams, a poor stenographer, and persuaded her to leave her home for him?

Richard was a young man, and the idea was not a surprising one to him. According to what he could learn, the dark-haired stenographer was fond of the things she could little afford to possess, and it was likely that her employer, knowing her desires, made it possible for her to gratify them.

Now that he was to marry, he would not be likely to hold out any inducement for the girl to stay with him, and if they should happen across her now it was possible that she would gladly return to the humble home of her sister.

Still, supposing Tolman Bike had found no attraction for him in the stenographer? It was a very delicate thing to handle, considering that Richard's knowledge was mostly supposition.

"Do you think that Maggie's sister really worked those nights she was away from home?" Dick asked Dido.

"She always brought extra money home, which proved she did," Dido replied positively.

"Did she ever talk about Tolman Bike?"

"Never, except when she mentioned that

he had dictated more work than usual, or something of that kind."

"Well, I believe that Tolman Bike can tell
me something about Maggie's sister," Richard
said.   Dido looked at him with a smile of
doubt.   "If she is not with him, he can tell
me who she is with, and that is just as well.
I must see him immediately.   I have no time
to lose, for three days from to-morrow he is to
be married."

CHAPTER XI.

WHO WAS THE MAN THAT BOUGHT THE GOWN ?

But Tolman Bike was not easily found.

Richard Treadwell got up early and went to the box factory, only to be told that Mr. Bike, suffering from ill-health, had gone out of the city for a time.

The people in charge of the shop either feigned ignorance or did not know when he was to return, but Dick knew, in view of Mr. Bike's approaching marriage, on the evening of the 7th, that he could not be absent from the city more than two days at the very most.

But one thing he determined on. He would see Tolman Bike before his marriage to Miss Chamberlain, and for Maggie Williams's sake he would know the whereabouts of her sister. And also for Maggie's sake would he do what he could for the sister to induce her to return to her home.

In the meantime Richard intended to make an extra effort to learn something about the Park mystery girl.

He drove to the Morgue, and after some persuasion he got the bundle of clothes the pretty dead girl had worn when found in the Park.

He took the gloves and gown and left the remaining articles with the keeper.

He decided from the appearance of the dress that it had been made at some expensive establishment. He further decided that he would make a round of the fashionable dress-making places and see if some one in them would not be able to recognize the work.

If they recognized the work, tracing the owner home should be very easy, he thought.

He took the gloves also, but like the dress, they had no mark that would assist him in his search.

After trying several glove stores he abandoned this as impracticable, for no one claimed the gloves as having been bought from them, and even if they had known the gloves were from their stock, it would have been impossible to tell who bought them.

Carefully he made a tour of the fashionable dressmakers. He felt dreadfully embarrassed as he entered the different establishments with the large parcel in his arms. The women in waiting, as well as the women customers, looked at him curiously, and when he asked, in a hesitating way, to see the proprietor or the forewoman, he could hardly endure the amused smiles of those who were eagerly listening to hear him state his business.

He thought all sorts of things which made him uncomfortable. First, the idea came to

him that they would think he had brought a
dress to be made to wear in amateur theatri-
cals, or at a masquerade. But that was not
half as bad as to imagine they thought he had
a wife who was displeased with a dress which
she had returned by him.

The worst part of all was, when he showed
the crumpled gown to the persons in charge
and inquired if they had made it, to have them
first show surprise at the unusual proceeding,
then quiet indignation when they found that
if Richard had a secret concerning the gown
he meant to keep it, and when he guarded
well his reasons for such a strange visit they
bowed him out with such an air of injured
dignity that Richard felt very small and
unhappy.

There were a few that instead of assuming
an injured air, laughed at Richard, and one
familiarly asked him if his wife refused to tell
where she got it.

The majority of the dressmakers denied the gown so emphatically that Richard began to have a dim idea that the workmanship was not so fine as had been thought and that the dress had come from a humbler shop. He, not being a woman, did not know that one dressmaker never saw any good in another dressmaker's work.

When he reached the last establishment of any note and importance it was almost dinner time. There were no customers about, and the employees were making preparations for closing the shop. A girl came forward and politely asked Richard his business.

He told her he wished to see whoever had charge of the place. Requesting him to be seated she left soon to return with a man.

Richard felt more comfortable than he had all day. He explained to the man, who listened kindly and politely, showing neither surprise nor curiosity, that he wished to find the persons who had made the gown he had with him, in order to find out who had paid for the dress and where it had been delivered.

The man took the gown and went to the workroom.   Later he returned and went inside the small office.

Richard waited impatiently, and for the first time a hope of solving the mystery of Central Park entered his heart.   Surely when the man took so much time he had discovered something.

Still Richard tried to keep his expectations from running away, lest he be compelled to suffer a severe disappointment; so when the man came towards him with the crumpled gown flung across his arm Richard offered the consolation to himself that he had still left for his inquiry the less fashionable dressmakers.

"The dress was made here," the man said. Dick's pulse started off at a two-minute gait.

"A letter was sent here containing an order for a dress. The measurements were inclosed and with them over half the price of the dress in bills. The letter stated that the person for whom it was intended was out of town, and that in ten days the dress·would be called for.

"We often have customers order dresses from a distance," the man continued, "and we make them from measure. Ten days afterwards a messenger boy came in with an order for us to receipt for the price of the dress and a $100 bill, from which I took the rest of the price and gave him the dress and the change."

"Have you the letter that was sent you with the measurements and order?" asked Richard, with a calmness that covered his excitement.

"No. The boy said he must have the letter containing the measurements, and I sent up to the forewoman in the workroom. She had transferred the order to her book, but had the letter pinned to the same page, so she sent it down and I gave it to the messenger."

" Have you not even the name and address of the person who ordered the dress?" asked Dick, very much cast down by the turn things had taken.

"The name we have—it was Miss L. W. Smith—but there was no address. It was an unusual thing for us to do, but as I told you, we have many customers who send us orders for dresses when they are away from town, and ladies are not always careful and exact about addresses. They are liable to fall into the error of thinking that if we have once made a garment for them, by merely signing their name we are sure to recall their address and histories. We keep very satisfactory books, which contain little histories of every garment we make, so we always refer to that when a lady forgets to write us as much as is necessary for us to know.

"Had you ever made a dress for Miss Smith before?" Dick asked, still a faint hope stirring his pulses.

"We thought so, but on consulting our books found the measurements showed that one was for a large woman and the other woman must have been slender."

"I suppose it is absurd to ask if you have any idea of where the messenger was from," Dick said, rather faintly.

"I do not know, of course, but there is a messenger office on the block above, where you might inquire. It is almost useless, though, for the lady doubtless got the boy in her district, and as you are aware, this is not a district of residences. Still, you would not lose anything by asking. They may be able to offer you some assistance. I can give you the date the boy called for the gown and I am very sorry I cannot do more for you."

The man had the gown put in a box for Richard, who left the establishment feeling happier than he had since he and Penelope had found the dead girl. He was on the track of her identity at last, and, though it was a a faint clue he possessed, he felt it a very sure one.

They did not show much inclination to help Richard at the District Telegraph office. At first they said it was impossible to tell which messenger it was, even if he had been from that place, and then, after a fashion, they did make a search, but with no success.

"I know it," said one of the messengers, who was standing at the counter. "I had stopped out front to scrap with Reddy Ryan, who was takin' a basket of clothes home, and a duffer drove up in a carriage and asked if I'd do a job for him, 'n I told him I'd been sent

on a call, so he said he'd give me a dime if I'd
run an' get him a messenger. I came, an'
Shorty, No. 313, was sent out. I remember it
'cause he told me the man just sent him into
Moscowitz's to get a dress an' pay a bill, an'
gave him a dollar for doin' it."

"Where is No. 313?" asked Dick, his
spirits rising fifty per cent.

"He's off on a call. No, here he is," said
the messenger who knew something. "Come
here, Shorty, you're wanted."

Shorty was a red-headed boy with a
freckled face and one eye. The other messenger recalled the circumstances to him, and
he sniffed his nose and said he remembered.

Richard then asked if there was a lady in
the carriage, but No. 313 thought not. Then
Richard asked him what the man looked like,
but No. 313 could not say, except that he had
a mustache and wore a soft felt hat. No.
313 had no opinion as to whether the carriage

was private or hired, but he "guessed" it wasn't a livery hack, "cause the harness jingled."

The other and brighter messenger said the man was young, denied the soft felt hat and pronounced the carriage a hired one.

    *   *   *   *   *

Richard hurried through his dinner, possessed of an unusual feeling of happiness, and went for Dido Morgan to spend their last evening in their peculiar search for Maggie's sister.

To-morrow Penelope would be home, and he had learned something. If ever so little, still it was something, and now that he had made such a successful start he began to feel hopeful of a final success. He knew now where the dress had been made and he knew a man had called for it. He had engaged the two messenger boys, and with them he intended to search the town over for the man who got the dress which the dead girl had worn. Once he found the man, then the rest would be easy.

Richard took Dido to the Eden Musée, and after she had seen all the figures that interested her, Dick took her up to the cosy retreat above the orchestra, where the tall green palms cut off the glare of the electric light. He ordered some ice cream for Dido and some Culmbacher for himself, and lighting a cigarette he gave himself up to the influence of the beautiful Hungarian music and dreams of Penelope.

The music sobbed and sighed, and Dick drifted on dream-clouds and was lazily happy. He would solve the mystery, he felt sure, and then what years of happiness with Penelope stretched before him. What a great thing it was to be happy ; life is so short, why should people allow themselves to be unhappy for a second if they can possibly avoid it ? An unusual tenderness filled his heart, a peaceful happiness stole over him, making him very gentle.

And poor little Dido, how dreary life loomed up before her! Dick's heart swelled with pity, and he sympathetically took the girl's hand in his and looked tenderly into the soft, brown eyes that looked at him so trustingly.

There was so much happiness and love in waiting for him and Penelope, but what did life offer to poor, lonely Dido?

And as the sobbing music ended in one long thrill, Richard, raising his eyes from the richly tinted face of this sweet girl companion, saw standing before him, with white face and stern eyes—

Penelope.

CHAPTER XII.

ONE AND THE SAME.

At the sight of Penelope Richard was dumfounded.

He stifled a first impulse to spring to his feet and greet her when he saw her stern, white and reproachful face, and sitting still tried slyly to drop Dido's hand.

With an almost imperceptible bow of recognition, Penelope went on after her aunt and a gentleman who, unnoticed, had in advance passed Dick and his companion.

"D—— it!" said Dick, warmly, in an undertone, and then he thought: "I'm in for it now. Penelope will never believe that thinking of my love for her made me feel a great pity for this lonely girl. She will say I was making love to her, because I held her hand, and she will never forgive it. What an ass I am to risk a life-time of happiness with Penelope, just to sympathize with a girl whose life is lonely, and yet, poor little devil— It's all up with Penelope, I know. I can tell by the look on her face that she will not forgive or believe me. I'll give up. It's no use now trying to solve the Park mystery—no use trying to do anything."

Dido looked uneasy. She had seen all and she partly understood. She said, in a little strained voice : " I am very sorry."

" I wish some man would tramp on my toes or punch me in the ribs. I'd just like a chance to knock the life out of somebody," Dick said, savagely.

Dido laughed softly at Dick's outburst, but she delicately avoided the subject of the lady who looked so angry.

"I forgot to tell you," she said, at length, in an effort to change the subject, "that it's all arranged at last."

"What?" asked Dick, curiously, the current of his thoughts leading him to think it was something about Penelope.

"Why, the affair between Maggie and Martin Shanks. Why, didn't you know?" in great surprise. "Why, I saw it all the first night you brought me back."

"I didn't notice anything in particular, but I recall plainly feeling Mr. Shanks in the dark," Richard replied, grimly. He always felt a little disgust at the remembrance of his fears that night, and he cherished a grudge against lanky Martin Shanks for waiting to be run over in the hallway.

"Well, Maggie and Martin are in love," exultingly.

"Possible!"

"Yes, and last night he proposed and was

accepted, and Sunday they are going to be married, and they are going down to Coney Island to spend the first day of their honeymoon," and Dido sighed in ecstasy.

"Lucky Martin, I'm sure; I wish I were in a like position," Dick said, half enviously, as the sad thought came that it was all over between him and Penelope. "I must get a nice present for Maggie."

"It was all so amusing," said Dido, with a rippling laugh. "I'm half sorry the courtship ended so soon. Martin was so faithful, so bashful, and so desperately in love. The only time he ever showed the least spirit was the night you took me home."

"I remember it quite well," Dick said, drily.

"I thought he was very insulting that night, but it's just his way, you know. He has liked you ever since then. You know he always stood guard in the hall; every night I was out, I would stumble over him, yet he couldn't be coaxed to come in. When Maggie took Blind Gilbert out to his stand, Martin always followed, so as to protect her coming home. Still, if she looked at him or spoke to him, he was so embarrassed that he couldn't answer."

"He gave her some flowers once, and when she thanked him, he was so broke up that he stammered that he had found them on Broadway and thought she might as well have them, and the great simpleton had bought them expressly for her. Next he bought some cloth for a dress, and when Maggie said she couldn't take it, he said he didn't want it, that he couldn't make any use of it. Just fancy Martin Shanks wearing a dress!"

Richard smiled at the picture presented to his mind of lanky Mr. Shanks in a gown.

"His proposal was the funniest thing," Dido continued, with a chuckle. "There came a loud knock on the door. Maggie opened it, and there before her was a work-basket. She picked it up and lifted the lid and there lay a plain gold ring."

"Martin," she said, going out to where he was standing in the hall, "you are too good to me. I can't take these things."

"I had an idee you'd let the parson, who brings us tracts, put that there ring on yer finger, and then you'd have the right to do me mendin'. It was an idee, maybe I'm wrong?"

"'Then Maggie said gently, 'Come in, Martin,' and he replied, 'If yu air wid me, Maggie?' and she blushed, and said, 'Yes, Martin,' and he stepped into the room, saying, 'I'll come in to settle accounts.'

"When he went out again all arrangements had been made for a speedy marriage. Martin said it was no use to waste time in being engaged, so they are to be married Sunday.

They are the happiest couple you ever saw," and Dido sighed enviously.

"And what is to become of you and blind Gilbert? Are you to have no share in their Eden?" Richard asked.

"Oh, yes. Maggie says they are going to rent a flat further uptown, and one room is to be for me and Lucille when she comes back, and Gilbert is to stay with them also. It's a pretty big family to begin with, but we'll all give what we can to pay expenses. I don't think Gilbert will go, though. He likes Maggie as though she was his daughter, but he's been so many years in that house on Mulberry Street that I don't think he will leave it."

"Well, this is our last evening to search for Maggie's sister," Richard said, with half regret, "and we have had no success whatever. I'm sorry, for Maggie's sake, though personally I feel it is just as well for her if her sister never returns to be a burden on her."

" I intend to see Tolman Bike before his marriage and learn from him where the sister is. Then, if we think it advisable, we can still persuade her to go home, but I have another important matter that will take all my time, so I cannot do much, for a while, at least, about Maggie's sister, unless Bike tells me where she is when I see him, as I intend to do to-morrow. I expect to be too busy working on an important case to see you for a while, but I hope your good luck will still continue, and you can congratulate Mr. Shanks and Maggie for me."

"It is useless for me to try to thank you for your kindness and help to me," Dido said, brokenly.

Dick's blue eyes beamed kindly on Dido as he replied, quickly: "There's a good girl, don't let us talk about that. I'm a useless fellow, and if I have been of the least service to any one, the gratitude is all on my side. I am grateful to you for allowing me to imagine I have been of service to you."

" You have been better to me than any one on earth," she said, vehemently, her eyes burning into his. " You have often said there was no gratitude in the world, so I won't say I would like to prove my gratitude to you, but some day—I'll wait. The day will come when I can show you what I feel."

" My dear child," he said, softly, his eyes moist, for he was much touched by the girl's words, " only be happy and that knowledge will make me happier."

Dido looked down and was silent. Presently two tears chased each other down over her cheeks and splashed on her slender hands, folded pathetically in her lap.

" Why, Dido, child !" Dick said, startled.

She raised her brown eyes, wet with tears, to his frank blue ones, and her lips were quivering pitifully. He took her hands, patting them soothingly, not daring to say a word.

" T-they *would* come," she faltered, her mouth bravely smiling while her eyes were filling with tears. " I—I could not help it."

He still said nothing, but kept on patting her hands, half embarrassed now.

" I was so—so wretched until you found me, and I've been so happy since, that—that I couldn't quite bear—your words."

" I hope I did not speak roughly," poor, blind Dick said, hardly understanding her grief. In his separation from her he was losing nothing, but she—poor child—she was losing everything.

" No—that's it. You are so kind," she faltered. " Don't, please, don't mind me. I am so foolish. I am always crying, don't you think ?"

She looked up at him with a sad, little smile that made his heart ache, he hardly knew why.

" Will you promise me something, Dido ?"
he asked, suddenly.

" Yes," she answered, simply.

" Promise that you will try to be happy;
that you will never cherish blue thoughts, no
difference what happens. Let ill-luck frown
on you all it wishes. Laugh at it ; laugh in it's
face until your laughter makes it smile.
Promise me to do this ?"

" Is that what you do ?" she asked, evasively.

" Well, I don't know. But what difference !
I don't get as low in spirits as you do. Won't
you promise ?"

" You have brought me happiness. I
promise if I get blue to think of you. Will
that do ?" she asked, seriously.

" I don't know," he said, half provoked,
but he urged no further.

And these two young people, whose barks
had floated side by side on the stream of life

for a brief time, were drifting apart. Mentally they were taking farewell, for they knew that, if even for a few days, they remained yet in sight or call, still their course lay so widely apart that they might never hope to float near each other again.

So they silently left the place where they had spent their last evening together and went out on the street into the cool quiet night.

A few gas jets dimly lighted up Twenty-third Street, and the stores that lined the opposite side frowned dark and gloomy upon the few people who occasionally made their appearance as they walked from the darkness into the light of the street lamps, and then disappeared again into the shadows beyond.

Coming towards the young couple from Sixth Avenue was a man, thoughtfully walking along, as if, unable to sleep, he had sought the quiet streets to think.

Richard noticed him, and pressing Dido's arm, he whispered :

" Look at this man."

"Yes, yes," she said, excitedly.'

The men exchange glances, and the stranger raised his hat stiffly in response to Richard's cordial greeting. After they had passed, Richard said :

"Why do you tremble so? I merely wanted to call your attention to him. That is Mr. Clarke, the gentleman I had the experience with in the Hoffman House bar."

" Mr. Clarke !" cried Dido, in amazement. " *Why that is Tolman Bike !*"

CHAPTER XIII.

A LOVERS' QUARREL

" Why !" as if unpleasantly surprised at his visit, " how do you do ?"

Such was Penelope Howard's greeting to Richard Treadwell the morning following the meeting in the Eden Musée. He could not stay away from her, so he decided to try to explain all about Dido. He wished now he had not been so anxious to keep the affair a secret until Penelope's return. It made things look all the blacker for him.

Penelope was a clever girl. She was bitterly hurt, but she had no intention of quarreling with Dick. If she experienced any jealous pangs he should not have the satisfaction of knowing it. She would merely maintain a cold indifference and make him feel that, do as he pleased, it was nothing to her. She would smile, but indifferently, and not with the smile of affection with which she had always greeted him. She would treat him in a manner that would show her displeasure and utter lack of affection for him, but she would not quarrel and so give him a chance to offer an apology or explanation.

"You don't seem very glad to see me ?" Dick ventured, with a forced smile.

Penelope looked with well assumed amazement and surprise at his audacity, and, raising her eyebrows, said with a slightly rising inflection, "No ?"

Richard felt very ill at ease.

"You don't understand," he continued, helplessly. "I hope at least you will allow me to explain the scene which you witnessed last night."

She said, with a cold smile : "Really, you must excuse me. I have no right or desire to know anything about your personal affairs."

"Confound it, Penelope. Don't be so infernally indifferent," exclaimed the young man with exasperation.

She simply looked at him. Scorn and disdain was pictured on her expressive countenance now.

" I hope Mrs. Van Brunt is well ?" he said awkwardly, hoping to bridge over Penelope's anger.

" Quite well, thank you," looking idly out the window.

" Is she at home ?"

" No ; she has just gone out with Mr. Schuyler," Penelope replied, picking up a book and aimlessly turning the leaves.

"I hope I may be permitted to call and pay my respects to her ?" he said, indifferently.

"Auntie will doubtless be pleased to see

you," was the reply, with a marked emphasis on the noun.

" How long are you going to keep up this nonsense, Penelope ?"

She shrugged her shoulders impatiently and pouted her lips, but made no reply.

" Do you know you are a very foolish girl sometimes ? You cheat yourself and me out of happiness. You know down in your heart you never doubt my faith to you. What pleasure you get from pretending that you do, I can't imagine. Come, be reasonable. Don't cultivate a bad temper."

" Hum ! I should not think you would care what I did if I am unreasonable, bad tempered, foolish, suspicious—is that all ?" mockingly. " I am glad to know your honest opinion of me. Doubtless, that cheap looking girl you were with last night is more amiable."

" I imagine she is, Penelope," Dick said, dejectedly and out of patience. " I have loved

you devotedly, and I have meekly endured all
your caprices, and if you want my devotion to
end in this way I can only obey. If you ever
regret it, Penelope, remember it was your own
doing. You sent me away and I shall not
return."

And Richard, a very wretched young man
indeed, walked hastily from the room.

Penelope never moved until she heard the
hall door close. She thought that he would
come back ; he always had, but when she realized that he had really gone she was surprised
and a little frightened.

Richard was very good-natured, but she felt
she had gone just a little too far, and that if
she wanted him back it would be necessary to
humble herself.

She could not recall a time before that she
had so forgotten herself, and allowed her temper to take such a hold of her. She could

hardly recall all she had said, but she felt very small and ungenerous.

Now that she had lost him she reviewed her own conduct, and felt that, although Richard had done wrong, she had been unnecessarily harsh. He deserved some punishment to teach him not to err again, but she had been too unforgiving.

Wasn't Dick always gentle and kind to her, and did he not always manfully and tenderly overlook her little mistakes and pettishness? Besides, was she not sure he loved her better than any girl in the world? Then why should she be jealous if he amused himself with those other women who are always so ready to " draw men on."

A woman in love always reproaches herself with being the cause of every lover's jar.

A woman in love invariably blames other women for all the slips made by the man she loves.

And they will do it to the end of the world.

While Penelope was spending the day racked with unhappy thoughts, Richard was busy trying to see Tolman Bike and managing the messenger boys in their search for the man who paid for the dead girl's gown.

Richard called at Mr. Bike's office, only to be informed that Mr. Bike was still absent from town. But he knew to the contrary this time ; so, obtaining the address, he called at Tolman Bike's bachelor apartments in Washington Square.

Mr. Bike was in town, this servant said, but he did not expect him in until it was time to dress for a 7 o'clock dinner. He did not know where Mr. Bike was to be found, so Richard was forced to rest content with this meagre information until a later hour.

Richard first consulted a directory. He found quite a list of Smiths, but no Miss L.

W. Smith, and he concluded if nothing more feasible offered he would select the Smiths who lived in the best neighborhoods, and personally visit every family until he found the right one, or knew positively no such Smith lived in New York. He had inserted a personal advertisement in all the morning and evening newspapers asking for information concerning the relatives of Miss L. W. Smith, and he expected by evening to have some definite clue to work on.

His disagreement with Penelope, instead of killing all desire to try further to solve the mystery of Central Park, infused him with new life and energy, and he was resolved to solve the mystery, and by doing so, make Penelope regret her unreasonableness.

Accompanied by the messenger boy, Richard Treadwell tried his original plan of walking about to meet people in the busy parts of the city.

"When you see a man that you think re-
sembles the man who got the dress, I want
you to tell me," he instructed the boy, and so
in hopes of knowing at least what the man
looked like, Richard spent the day wearily
travelling around.

"There goes a fellow that looks just like
the other duffer," the boy announced, as he
and Dick stood watching the passers-by on
Broadway.

Richard started to follow the man who, in
company with a red-headed florid-faced man
that carried about with him one hundred and
fifty pounds of superfluous flesh, was going
down Broadway.

The man pointed out by the boy had a
light beard, a high nose and sharp eyes.
Richard recognized him as an Albany assem-
blyman.

"That looks totally unlike the man I pictured from your description," Richard said,

crossly, as they followed the two men into the Hoffman House.

"Well, his face looks like the other fellow, only the other one had black whiskers, and this here one's is red."

"Bleached, doubtless," Dick said ironically.

"Well, he looks the same, anyway," the boy protested, as Dick seated himself in the bar-room and made a pretense of reading a letter.

The two men went to the bar and ordered drinks, and as the thinner one (they were neither on the lean order) raised a glass to his mouth, Richard started and looked more closely at him.

Surely his face looked familiar then !

"I am tired ; you can go to your office now and come to me in the morning," Dick said to the messenger, who gladly started off.

Richard sat there with serious face watching

the man at the bar whom the boy had pointed out, until he and his heavy companion went out ; then Dick fell into deep thought.

A wild, improbable suspicion had come to his mind, so improbable, so wild, that he felt ashamed to dwell on it. The likeness was familiar; so unlike, and yet so strangely like, that Dick hardly knew what to believe.

" Poor devil ! Why should I allow a chance resemblance to make me accuse him of a thing so bad as that. He has enough to bear and answer for now, yet—yet— But it's too wild, too improbable. I'll forget it, I'll dismiss the thought from my mind ; the messenger was surely mistaken, and I'll devote my evening to seeing about Maggie's sister. Here's to an evening free from all thoughts of that dead girl. And yet—it's very strange—I half believe "— Then, shrugging his shoulders, Dick impatiently drained his glass and started for Washington Square.

CHAPTER XIV.

"GIVE ME UNTIL TO-MORROW."

As Richard was early, he stopped for a moment to see Dido Morgan, and finding her ready to start home, asked her to walk a little way with him down Fifth Avenue.

She was looking quite wan when he went in, but she brightened up and flushed with pleasure at the prospect of seeing him for a little time.

"I had an offer from a manager to-day to go on the stage," she said, quietly.

"I hope you did not accept it," Dick replied, quickly, looking at the girl's downcast face, which seemed strangely altered since last night.

"Not yet."

"And you won't, Dido?" he said, pleadingly.

"I don't see why not, Mr. Treadwell."

Dick started unpleasantly. He had not
before noticed that she never called him by
any name when addressing him, and now it
seemed to suggest that there was a difference
between them, and he vainly wondered what it
was.

"I should be very sorry, Dido, to see you
go on the stage. In the first place you don't
know anything about acting, and it would take
you years before you could hope to attain any
position."

"I FEEL that I can act," she said deeply.
"My nerves seem so tight that I long to get
up and act some life. I want to act love, and
then hate, and then murder."

"Why, Dido?" Dick asked, coolly and
curiously, although he felt the deep emotion
underlying her words. He recalled what an

old club-man said to him once, that every
woman disappointed in love wanted to act, and
he half wondered if Dido had been falling in
love with some of the handsome men who fre-
quented photograph galleries to have repro-
duced the being they love most of any on
earth, but he put away the thought as a wrong
to Dido.

"I *feel* it, I tell you I feel it. I can't
endure a monotonous life any more. I must
have some excitement," she said, passionately.

"I tell you what you want—exercise! You
want to walk and you want to swing clubs and
you'll soon be all right. You are so confined
that you have a superfluous energy which your
work does not exhaust. If you spend it on
exercise, it will make you a happier and
stronger girl."

Dido showed a little resentment. It
always disgusts a woman to have her romantic
feelings dissected in a matter-of-fact manner.

Having reached Washington Square, she bade Richard good-bye and went on her way to her humble home.

Richard walked along North Washington Square until he came to the house where he expected to find the man who had taken Lucille Williams from her home. He went up one flight of stairs to Tolman Bike's apartments, and knocked on the door on which was tacked Mr. Bike's visiting card.

In a moment the door was opened, and the man he knew as Mr. Clarke stood before him.

" Mr. Bike," said Richard, with emphasis on the name, " I must speak with you alone."

Richard spoke imperatively and at the same moment stepped inside.

Mr. Bike looked as ill as the day he fell against the Hoffman House bar. He silently motioned Dick to enter the first room leading off the private hall in which they stood. Closing and locking the door he followed.

Richard seated himself in an easy chair, unasked. Mr. Bike sat down before a richly-carved desk, littered with packages of letters and photographs, which apparently he had been engaged in assorting and destroying, for bundles of them were slowly smouldering in the open grate.

The room was very handsome, and Richard viewed it with appreciation. There was a large open grate and above the low, wide mantle was a cabinet containing, in the centre, a French plate mirror, and on the brackets fine bits of bric-a-brac. The floor was richly carpeted, the walls were hung with fine paintings, while near the portiéres, draped just far enough back to give a picturesque perspective view of a suite of rooms as cosy in the rear, was an alabaster statue of The Diver and another of Paul and Virginia.

A Mexican *serape*, quaintly colored, was thrown over a low lounge, before which lay a

white fur rug. At one side was a little, square
breakfast table, with curiously turned legs, and
near it a half side-board, half cabinet, attrac-
tively filled with exquisite dishes, a few solid
silver pieces and crystal glasses, backed up by
long-necked bottles of liquids to fill them.

Mr. Bike had removed his coat and waist-
coat and had on a little embroidered jacket.
He did indeed have an unhealthy pallor, and
Dick noticed that the hand with which he
toyed with a carved paper-cutter shook
violently.

"How this man loves life and its good
things," Dick thought, sympathetically, as his
gaze wandered from one article of luxury to
another, and on to another room, where, just
through the portiére, he could see a brass cage,
in which a yellow canary was jumping restlessly about, and a small aquarium, up through
which came a spraying fountain. He could
even see goldfish swimming about and a little

dark turtle run its head out of the water and then dive down again to the bottom of the basin.

"I suppose you know why I came to see you?" Dick said at last, when he saw Mr. Bike would not introduce any subject.

"No, I can't say that I do," Mr. Bike responded, with affected indifference.

"Well, I want to know all about Lucille Williams," he said abruptly

"What right have you to come to me for such information?" Mr. Bike asked coldly.

"Because you induced the girl to leave her home," Dick replied positively, "and I want to know all you have to tell about the rest of it."

"I have nothing to tell," Mr. Bike said, with a slight, sarcastic smile.

"Well, sir, if you won't tell, I'll find a way to make you," Richard said, angrily.

" Ah! Indeed!" Mr. Bike ejaculated, still cool and unconcerned.

" Yes, sir ; if you don't tell me what I want to know before I leave here, I will go to Miss Chamberlain, your fiancée "—Mr. Bike started uneasily—" I'll tell her a story you would not like her to know."

" And you flatter yourself that she would believe you ?" sarcastically.

" I know it. I can prove what I have to say," Dick replied in a manner that was unmistakable.

" All right, go to her. See what you can do."

" By Jove, I will. I will go to the newspapers too, and I'll tell them—"

" What ?" Mr. Bike asked, rather uneasily.

" You know *what !* Disabuse your mind of any idea that I don't know some chapters in your life, that, if made public, will end your devilish career." Richard hinted darkly, the suspicions which had come to him before that day sweeping over him with full force.

Tolman Bike was thinking intently. Richard saw that his last bluff had gone home and he determined to follow it up with more of the same kind.

"Be as unconcerned as you please, Mr. Bike. To-morrow, when your marriage is postponed, and you are called on to answer to the serious charge I shall bring against you, you will be sorry that you didn't take the easier course, and give me the information I asked for." Dick said this as if his patience had run out.

"I have no information to give," Mr. Bike said, in a tone which showed he was beginning to weaken.

"Say, it's wasting time to pretend to me. Either you will, or you will not, do as I have asked you. If you don't, the consequences be on your own head."

" And would you—do you mean—" hesi-
tated Tolman Bike, losing confidence at sight
of Dick's undiminished determination.

"Yes, sir ; I mean every word of it."
Dick had risen and he looked very angry and
capable of doing all the bad things he threatened. " I have given you a chance, and you
refuse to accept, so—" and he shrugged his
shoulders as if his responsibility ended there.

" And if you get the information, what use
will you make of it ?" asked Bike, as if longing
for some hope to be held out to him.

"You know what I want. It is not to
bring any credit to myself, but to relieve the
suspense of a heart-broken sister."

" And would you, if I tell you all, be man
enough to show some mercy ?" he asked, in a
hopeless way.

" I hold out no promises. I am determined
to have a confession from you before your
marriage. If you don't give it, you don't

marry, and you can put that down for a cer-
tainty," Dick said doggedly.

"And if I tell you," in sudden hope, "will
you let my marriage go on without telling
Clara? Promise to let us get away on our
wedding tour and then you can do as you
wish. Only give me that much," almost
pleaded the now trembling man.

"And let you wreck the life of the innocent, unsuspecting woman who becomes your
bride? What sort of a man do you think I
am?" Richard asked in scorn.

"My God, man! Have some feeling.
Haven't I suffered enough already? You are
a man, you can understand how a man will
sell his soul to hell for the sake of a woman,"
he said bitterly. "Have some feeling!"

"Can't you understand it?" he continued,
desperately, in vain effort to wake compassion
in Richard's breast. "She was pretty, she

had no friends to make any trouble about it, and I lost my head.   I have suffered for it. I have regretted it."   And Tolman Bike put his hands over his face, and Richard heard a broken, husky sob.

This was more than he could endure.   His sternness fled at that sound, and he could hardly refrain from attempting to console the wretched man.   Only thoughts of the poverty-stricken little sister helped him maintain an air of unrelenting sternness.

"Well, what do you ask of me?" Richard asked with a roughness that covered his real feeling.   Now that he had conquered the man his suspicions fled.   He felt sorry for Bike's suffering and had a guilty feeling that he was the cause of it.

"Only give me until to-morrow and I'll swear to you that you shall know what you want to before ten o'clock.   Give me until then.   If I fail, you have yet time to stop my

marriage in the evening. You are a man, but
if you won't spare me for a man's follies, spare
me for the sake of the woman I am to marry.
I'm sick ! I can't talk ! Only give me until to-
morrow."

" —— it, Bike," Richard said, feelingly,
" if it wasn't for the girl's sister, I'd fling the
whole thing over." He little knew what it
meant to him. " I believe your promise. I'm
a man, reckless, indolent, careless as the worst
of them, and, confound it, I'm sorry for you.
There's my hand."

" Thank you, thank you," Bike said, his
deep emotions showing in the painful twitch-
ing of his pale face. He clasped Dick's firm
hand in his own dry, feverish one, and gave it
a grateful pressure.

" Until to-morrow, then ?"

" Until to-morrow," echoed the unhappy
man. looking into Dick's face with an appealing look of agony that Richard never forgot.

CHAPTER XV.

"TO RICHARD TREADWELL, PERSONAL."

It was ten o'clock when Richard Treadwell in gown and slippers, sat down in a high-backed chair to partake of a light breakfast.

The dainty table was spread with its burden of light rolls and yellow butter, with a bit of ice on it, and crisp, red berries. The odor of the coffee was very appetizing, but Richard ate and read the morning paper at the same time.

The awnings lowered over the windows shut out the glare of the morning sun. A light breeze moved the curtains lazily, and a green palm on the window-sill waved its long arms energetically, as if to hurry the indolent young man who was missing the beauty of Summer's early morning.

Richard Treadwell's rooms were as unlike the elegant apartments of Tolman Bike, as a violet is unlike a rose. One, like a laughing, romping child, denoted health and cheerfulness ; the other, unhealthy in tone and coloring, spoke of dreams and selfish gratification.

Here were copies of Rosa Bonheur's master-pieces of animal life, pictures of racing horses, photographs of serious-faced dogs in comical positions, a stuffed fish's head, with wide open mouth, mounted on a plaque ; boxing gloves, clubs and dumb-bells, lying where they had fallen after this young man had taken a turn at each of them. There was an unsorted jumble of walking-sticks, whips, fishing tackle and firearms. The furniture was light, the curtains were thin and airy, the carpet was bright and soft.

Richard ate and read unmindful of the wrestling match between a bow-legged pug and a saucy black-and-tan, whose little sharp ears stood stiffly erect, expressive of cool amusement at the fat pug's futile attempts to throw him.

As Richard pushed his chair back and lighted a cigarette, a man-servant entered quietly and put a large envelope and a smaller one on the table before him. Richard took the larger envelope and read the superscription.

To

RICHARD TREADWELL, ESQ^{RE}.

FROM   *PERSONAL.*

     TOLMAN BIKE.

He hastily tore it open with his thumb. The letter began without any preliminaries:

In writing this I place my life at your disposal. I neither expect mercy nor ask it.

I have been so wretched for days that life is a burden I little care to bear.

Do what you please with this, but if you possess an unheard-of generosity I would ask you, after clearing yourself, to spare me as much as possible.

" My wild, improbable suspicions were correct !" Dick exclaimed, in surprise. The black-and-tan, hearing his voice, came and jumped inquiringly against his knee, but receiving no attention returned to finish the English Kilrain on the rug.

I first met Lucille Williams when she came to my office in answer to my advertisement for a typewriter and stenographer. Of the many who applied I selected her. Not because she was the most proficient worker, but for a man's reason.

She had a pretty face.

Wonderfully pretty, I have had men tell me. She had large, clear blue eyes and an abundance of wavy black hair, and a faultless pink and white complexion that often accompanies the combination. Her hands were small and slender. She was particular in the care of them, and her remarkably small feet were always well shod.

Life is dull at best during business hours, so I amused myself with my pretty typewriter. It started first by my playfully putting my arm around her chair when dictating. Harmless enough. Yes, but it brought me so close to her that I began to wonder what she would do if I kissed her. When I stopped in my dictation she raised her great, blue, alluring eyes to me in such a way, that I wouldn't have been a man had I not felt a little thrill of temptation.

I did kiss her at last.

She was not much offended. She cried a little and wanted to know what she had done that encouraged me to insult her. Her chief fault was vanity, so I pleased myself and comforted her by taking her in my arms and vowing that the sight of her red lips so close, and her great eyes, so alluring and entrancing, was more than I could resist. It comforted her and pleased me.

Yes, I said something of love.

It somehow seemed the only thing to say under the circumstances. I think I called her "My Love," and similar names. I am positive I did not say that I loved her, although I recall coaxing her to say she loved me.

She said she loved me and I believed her.

It was all very pretty and interesting while it had the charm of newness. We soon spent our evenings together. I took her to restaurants patronized by Bohemia, where, if one happens across an acquaintance, he, on a similar errand, is just as anxious to keep it a secret as you are. In the summer, when there was less chance of embarrassing meetings, I took her to better places and occasionally to the theatre.

I found it interesting.

Meanwhile, I learned that Lucille's sister was employed in the factory, and I threatened Lucille with an eternal parting if, by any chance, her family learned of our intimacy. When the pretence of seeing friends and persons about business would no longer serve as a blind, I instructed Lucille to say she was engaged on extra work. She very sensibly said she could not do this without money to show for it, so I promptly made it possible. Thereafter that was her blind.

Thus she deceived her family.

Meanwhile I thought I would feel more comfortable if Lucille were better dressed. You know how men feel on this subject. Most of them would rather be seen in company with the lowest woman in New York if she wore a Paris gown, than with a woman in rags, even if she were as pure as a saint. A man is always afraid of being chaffed for being with a badly dressed woman.

For the world, looking on, judges only by the dress.

I spoke to Lucille. I found she was as sensitive about her cheap garments as I was, so I told her if she would buy an entire outfit suitable for our wanderings I would pay for it. I made suggestions, and the garments she bought were as lady-like and appropriate as if it had been an every-day affair with her.

Then came the question, Where to send the clothes?

She could not send them home, for her mother and sister, though poor, had Puritan ideas concerning morals and propriety.

There is a way out of every difficulty.

I had her send all her new articles to my bachelor apartment. Then I gave her a key, so she could enter my rooms at any time to change her cheap clothing for her new and vice versa.

So I got her to my rooms.

I don't deny that it was my intention at first to finally take her there, but I wanted to preserve the sentiment of the affair as long as possible. She was very perfect to the sight, very lovable, and I was eager for our evenings—anxious to drip out as slowly as possible the intoxication of the affair, still breathlessly eager to drain the cup.

There is no need of going into detail.

You know what bachelor apartments are; you know what opportunities they afford. Lucille was timid at first; afraid to come in or go out, but she soon grew bolder. She even grew to like the danger of it.

I was very fond of her then.

There is no use to be hypocritical and cry it was love of her that led me on. Why men adopt such weak pleas, I never could understand.

It was not love of her.

A man never injures a woman through love of her, but through love of self. I realized this all the time, but I was passionately happy, and happiness is not so plentiful that I should slight it, result as it might.

I promised to marry her.

It happened in a moment when I loved her best. I knew at the time, I was doing a reckless thing. The next day I warned her to keep our love secret, because there were reasons why, if it were known, it would be injurious to me. She, appreciating the difference between us, was as silent as I could be.

By and by things began to pall.

I was too well acquainted with her. I grew tired of her pretty face. Her little vulgarities exasperated me. She was a woman of such little variety, and she so weakly bowed to every demand I made that it became unbearable.

I have known homely women whose charms were more lasting.

Her weakness maddened me. I grew to hate her. If she had only had enough spirit to quarrel with me, but that was the secret of it; she had no spirit until it was too late.

Just before this I met Miss Chamberlain. I found that I had pleased her fancy and I concluded to marry.

It mattered little that I was not in love; I had long since learned that love was merely the effect of some pleasing sensation, which some persons, like some music, produce on us, that shortly wears itself out.

I thought it better to marry where there was no feeling than where there was. For the sensation of love is sure to die, leaving an unsupportable weariness caused by its own emotion. Where there is no such feeling, there is no such result to fear.

I never expected any trouble from Lucille.

But I reckoned without my host. Although I endeavored to keep my engagement secret, yet a line to the effect that I was to marry Miss Chamberlain, reached print. Lucille, though hardly in society, always read society notes. She read that one.

She became a tigress—a devil. Isn't it queer that a weak woman always has an ungovernable temper? Expecting nothing more than a few tears from her, I answered carelessly, and she grew infuriated. Of course, I was astonished. She accused me of falseness and demanded that I deny the report over my own name and marry her immediately, or she would seek Miss Chamberlain and lay before her what she pleased to call my baseness.

I was determined to marry.

It meant wealth, a better social position, power, and a wife that at least I would be proud of. I had cherished such an idea of marriage since I was a boy, and I was resolved that nothing should balk me now that it was in my grasp.

I was determined to take fate into my own hands.

Finding I could not quiet Lucille, I concluded to rid myself of all responsibility in her case.

Call me base if you will !

Was I doing more than hundreds of men are doing in New York to-day !

Had I done more than hundreds—aye, thousands—of men have done in New York ?

You are a man of education and means ; denounce me if you have never sinned likewise.

Let any New York man of education, leisure and money denounce me, if any there are who have not likewise blundered.

It was only a matter of a few days' amusement, harmless if it ended quietly.

But I slipped up on it—therein lies the sin. Not in what I did, but in blundering over it.

People may say what they will. I was not wrong. It is the system that is wrong, the system that prevents people who care for each other from being happy in that affection while it lasts. Had the system been different Lucille would have been home to day, happier and in more comfortable circumstances than previous to our meeting, and I—I would not now be writing to you.

But there was nothing to save us.

Tired and disgusted with Lucille, she further exasperated me with her jealousy and unreasonable demands for a speedy marriage. Fearful of losing the marriage which meant so much to me, I carefully planned what seemed the only course to pursue.

Yes, it was deliberate.

Calming her anger for the day, I persuaded her to come to my apartment—these very

rooms where I sit and quietly write this confession of my crime.

Unsuspecting, aye, even gladly she came—
came to meet her fate, which waited for her
like a spider in his entangling web for a fly.

" If you please, sir, Miss Howard's compli-
ments, and would you come up as soon as
possible," said a voice at the door.

The little black-and-tan paused for a moment, with the pug's ear still between his little
sharp teeth, to see where the voice came from,·
and Richard responded, impatiently : " Very
well, say I'll be there," and returned to Tolman
Bike's letter.

CHAPTER XVI.

THE MYSTERY SOLVED.

The mockery of the thing amused me.

I knew so well how it was to end, and when Lucille came cheerfully to me, never thinking but that she would return to her home that night, I laughed aloud.

She wanted to talk about my promise of marriage, and I readily consented. In very few words I gave her to understand that it was impossible for me to marry her in her present condition, but if she would be guided by my judgment, and bought suitable clothing, we could then go away and be quietly married. To do this it was necessary that she remain with me.

She was more than satisfied.

She was elated over her brilliant prospects. Still she was stubbornly determined to notify her family, and only by threatening to abandon the whole affair if it became known did I keep her from doing so. I did, however, consented to her writing a note saying she had gone out of town for a few weeks, and on her return would have a joyful surprise for them. It satisfied her and did not hurt me.

The letter was never mailed.

Lucille's presence was not unknown to some few. My servant, who slept at home, knew I had somebody with me, but as he had served many years in taking care of bachelor apartments, he was neither surprised nor inquisitive. The waiters who served our meals knew I was not alone, but to them, also, it was a story too old to merit comment. Still I took precautions that they should not see Lucille.

In the garments I had bought her I sent

Lucille to a dressmakers to get her measurements. I also sent her to a dentist to have some decaying teeth filled, and so I started to work out my release from a woman of whom I had tired.

You might say that I could have taken a more simple way. I don't see how. I was afraid of losing my wealthy fiancée and so I would not risk the least chance of Lucille's telling. Of course I could have claimed blackmail and been declared innocent, yet, knowing the nature of the woman I was hoping to marry, I would not risk the effect it would have on her.

There seemed only one thing to do, and I did it. I had Lucille write an order for a dress, from my dictation, inclosing the measurements and stating that it would be called for on a certain date. Personally I went to different stores and bought the garments necessary to make a perfect outfit. I did not spare expense. I brought everything home with me in the coupé. This relieved me of necessity of giving any address or name, which made me feel sure the articles could not be traced to their destination.

During this time Lucille was very happy, notwithstanding her imprisonment. She was constantly planning what she would do when we were married. She dwelt in delight on the sensation her marriage would create among those who knew her. She discussed the localities most suitable for us to live in, and talked of things she intended to buy for her house and the dresses she meant to get.

It is useless to try to describe the emotions I labored under during those days. I was conscious of a tiredness, underlaid with a stolid determination not to be balked in my purpose. I felt no sympathy for Lucille. I think I was absolutely without feeling one way or the other. I only felt a desire to laugh at

her air castles as she told them to me. Not
amused—no. I can't say what the feeling
was. Even when she lay awake some nights
and I knew she was painting her future, I
laughed aloud at the strangeness of it all.

I counted the nights. Every one found
my preparations nearer completion.

Carefully I removed all trade marks and
names from every garment I had bought her.
The gloves and *Suéde* shoes only bore their
size. I took the crown lining out of the hat,
and before I brought her dress home I removed
the inside belt, which was stamped with the
name of the man who made it.

The dress was the last article but one I
brought to my apartment. I did not even
show myself at the establishment where the
gown was made. I drove near the place, and,
hiring a messenger boy, sent him in for the
garment. In this way I preserved the secret
of my identity.

The last thing I bought was a bottle of hair bleaching fluid. I told Lucille that if her hair was golden to match her eyes I thought her appearance would be much improved. She was quite anxious to make the test, always being ready to do anything she thought would increase her beauty. For two days, at different intervals, I brushed her hair with the fluid, and it turned the most perfect golden shade I had ever seen.

It really transformed her. I have since then marvelled at the change and have felt an admiration for her perfect beauty. Then I felt nothing.

I only had a desire to watch her. I watched her eat and wondered at her appetite. I listened to her light talk and marvelled at her happiness. I gazed at her while she slept, amazed, almost, at her evident sense of security.

Why did nothing warn her? I waited and watched for some sign that would show that instinct felt the approaching end. There was no sign.

The last night, I leaned on my elbow and watched her sleep. She looked so perfect! Her soft, dimpled arms thrown above her head, her pretty face in a nest of golden hair, her straight black brows, her long, black lashes resting lightly on her pink cheeks, and all to become nothing—nothing. To-morrow night it would be over; this was her last night. Impulsively I leaned over her and whispered " Lucille ! Lucille !" but she merely opened her great blue eyes, and giving me a little smile, as innocent and sweet as a babies, moved with a sigh of perfect content close to my arm, which rested on the pillow, and so went to sleep again.

I lay down and tried to still the heavy,

painful beating of my heart. I was very weary, but I could not sleep.

At breakfast something kept saying, " Her last ! her last !" and it gratified me to see her eat. At luncheon she complained of no appetite, yet I almost compelled her to eat, while I ate nothing. During the day I told my servant to take a holiday, that I would be out of town and he could have several days to spend as he wished. Rid of him, I ordered a dinner fit for a wedding feast ; still I could not eat. Lucille ate and I helped her joyfully. I had a desire to see her happy. I have thought the jailer who feasts the condemned prisoner an hour before the execution must feel as I felt this day.

Late in the evening I laid her new garments, the finery that so delighted her, out on the bed. I laughed when I did it, and then I sat down and watched her dress. She was as happy as a child. She put on one thing after the other, surveying each addition in the mirror with little cries of delight. I laced her *Suéde* shoes and helped fasten her dress and buttoned her gloves. When all was done I wrapped her in a gray travelling cloak and hid her pretty face under a thick veil.

I had told her we would take the midnight train for Buffalo, where we would be married, and remain at Niagara for a few days before our return to New York. She trusted me in everything, and asked me if she could increase her wardrobe before the time for our return. We were to start early enough to permit us to take a drive before going to the station. Lucille had been confined so long in the house that she welcomed this arrangement, and she was very eager and nervous to start.

I had ordered my horse and dog-cart to be ready at a certain hour. I had a liking for late drives, so my orders were not considered unusual. I walked out of the house, first telling Lucille to lock the door and walk around the corner on Fifth Avenue, where I would get her.

Before starting, however, I asked Lucille to drink a glass of wine with me. I put in hers a sleeping potion, and she raised it to her lips, saying :

"Here's to our happiness."

I put my wine down untasted.

Then she came to me in an affectionate way I had once admired, and raising her veil, said :

"Tolman, kiss your little one."

I folded her in my arms. My heart beat quickly, my breath came painfully. I held her close to my breast, I kissed her soft, warm, lips regretfully.

"Lucille," I said, pleadingly, "will you go back to your home and forget you wanted to be my wife ?"

"I would rather die," she answered me, angrily.

I knew then it was too late. There was no way to retreat. Either I must accomplish my purpose, or renounce all claim to Miss Chamberlain and take Lucille as my wife.

"We have been very happy these two weeks, haven't we, Tolman?" she said, with her arms about my neck. "Kiss your little one good-by, for when she comes back here she will be your wife."

"Yes, when you come back," I said, and I kissed her. With that there flitted through my mind a picture of a little quiet home with her as my wife. I thought of her beauty, but then came the thought that it would cost me what I most longed for—wealth—position. No, it was too late.

I drove to the curb almost the instant she had reached there, and only stopped long enough to get her in. I had a valise, which

Lucille thought contained a change of clothing, in the dog-cart.   I drove off quickly to the
Park.

We had not more than entered the Park
when Lucille yawned and complained of
feeling drowsy.   I drove on, listening intently
for any sounds that would indicate the presence of any one.   Reaching a bend in the
road and finding everything still, I asked
Lucille to hold the reins until I could get out
to see if something was not amiss with the
harness.

Drowsily she took the reins.

"Do you see anything coming, Lucille?"
I asked, as I reached under the seat and,
drawing out a sandbag which I had made ready
in advance and concealed there, I rose to my
feet as though to jump out of the buggy.

"No, Tolman; the way looks clear," she
replied. slowly, as she leaned forward to
look.

With a swift motion I raised the sandbag and brought it down on her head.

She never uttered a sound, but fell across the side of the cart. I caught her with one hand and, taking the reins from her limp fingers, steadied the horse.

I took her in my arms to the nearest bench. I listened for her heart-beats. They were still. I removed the Connemara cloak and veil. I had some difficulty, but at last managed to place her in an upright position on the bench. Then I folded her hands in her lap, and as I could not make her parasol stay on her knee, I left it where it fell on the ground before her.

I kissed her lips, still warm and soft, and closing her eyes, pulled her hat down so it would prevent their opening. Taking the wrap and veil and putting them and the sandbag in the valise I drove back to the stable.

I returned to my rooms and spent the remainder of the night in destroying all the clothing which belonged to her. Early in the morning, just about daybreak, I went quietly out and to the Gilsey House, where I got a room and went to bed. I slept. It was afternoon when I awoke, and while eating my breakfast I read in the first edition of an evening paper an account of your finding Lucille's body in Central Park.

In the smaller envelope I enclose a photograph of Lucille taken before her hair was bleached. You will doubtless recognize it. I also inclose the letter she wrote to her mother.

You can understand now why I was frightened at the sight of Maggie Williams's tears ; why I was horrified when I met in the Hoffman House the man who was suspected of being guilty of my crime. My guilty fears prevented my giving you my name, and when you came to my apartment, seeking Lucille, I knew that my hour had come.

I might have given you a fight and warded off the end for a while. But what use. If the proof was not conclusive enough to hang me, it was enough to imprison me, for the waiters, my servant and the livery-man could have made out a case of circumstantial evidence. I prefer death.

It is morning. The morning of the day which was to have been my wedding day. Oh God, I had some wild hope when I began this confession. It has gone now. This is all. If you have any charity in your soul, spare me all you can.

TOLMAN BIKE.

NORTH WASHINGTON SQUARE,

June Seventh, 18—.

CHAPTER XVII.

SUNLIGHT THROUGH THE CLOUDS.

Richard could hardly dress quickly enough
after he finished Tolman Bike's letter. The
indolent young man had never been seen in
such frantic haste. The elevator seemed to
him to creep. Rushing out to the street, he
jumped into the first cab, telling the driver to
make the best possible speed to Fifth Avenue.

With a sad, penitent face, Penelope Howard was impatiently awaiting her handsome
lover in her own little room, her abject apolo-
gies all cut and dried for use. But he gave
her no time.

" Penelope, the mystery is solved!" he
yelled, and catching her in his strong arms, he

held her so close to his heart that she gasped for breath.

" I've the story right here, sweetheart," and in the fewest possible words, punctuated with Penelope's exclamations of surprise and sorrow, Richard related all that had happened since the night before she went to Washington.

" My dear—Oh, Richard. Good morning," said Penelope's aunt, as she entered the room with bonnet on and a carriage-wrap thrown hastily over a house dress. " Mrs. Chamberlain has sent for me. They have just received news that Clara's fiancée, Mr. Bike, was found dead in his bathroom, shot through the head. They think it was accidental, and poor Clara, who was to have been a bride this evening, is prostrated. I'll be back presently, dear. Richard stay with the child."

They let her go without a word of the information they possessed, and, oblivious to all else, they read Tolman Bike's confession.

Woman-like, Penelope was in tears, and had as much pity for the unhappy man as for the luckless girl.

"I knew he was the man," Richard said. "When the messenger boy pointed out the man in the Hoffman House as looking like the man who got the gown, the resemblance struck me, though this man was fair and Tolman Bike was dark. The moment the resemblance struck me, the whole thing flashed before my mind. My ridiculous remark that probably the man was bleached, suggested to me the possibility of Maggie's sister having bleached after she left home. Still, it was all so wild and improbable that I tried not to think of it."

They decided only to tell the secret of the crime to those most concerned. That done, they effectually saved the name of Tolman Bike from deeper disgrace., little as he deserved it.

When Mrs. Van Brunt returned from the

house where the preparations for wedding fes-
tivities had been turned into arrangements for
a funeral, Penelope, with her eyes red from
weeping, drew her aunt into her own little den
where Richard was. Together they told the
astonished woman the story of the crime, and
she was more determined even than they were
that the confession should be held sacred, since
making it public could benefit no one, and
would only serve to hurt the family who had
expected to welcome him into their home as
the husband of the daughter of the house.

They had intended to visit Maggie Williams that day and tell her the story of her
sister, but Mrs. Van Brunt, more thoughtful,
told them to delay the sad information until
the girl was married, as Richard had told them
of her intended marriage Sunday.

Tolman Bike was privately buried Sunday
from the Chamberlain mansion, while the girl
who was to have been his bride, lay uncon-

scious in a darkened room upstairs.   Mrs. Van
Brunt, as an old and intimate friend of Mrs.
Chamberlain, went to the funeral.   Penelope
went with her aunt, her heart divided in sympathy for the dead man, the dead girl, and the
stricken daughter of the Chamberlain house-
hold.   If Tolman Bike had lived, Penelope
would have hated him for his crime, but
because he had strength to die, and when she
pictured his lonely end, she felt sorry for his
wretched fate.

Sunday evening they visited Maggie Williams, now Mrs. Martin Shanks, and Penelope
gently told them the story of the Mystery of
Central Park, omitting as much as possible
that would pain the sister.   Rough, but kindly
Martin Shanks comforted his bride.   Dido
Morgan mingled her tears with Maggie's, but
she was shy and awkward, having little to say
in the presence of Penelope Howard, though

Penelope did her utmost to be cordial and con-siderate.

The warm, frank feeling that had hereto-fore existed between Dido and Dick was gone. Dick endeavored to be friendly and pleasant, but Dido maintained a stiff silence that made him have a sense of relief when he and Penelope finally took their departure.

"Ah, Penelope, it's true, as Tolman Bike said, happiness is not so plentiful in life that we can afford to let it slip by when near our grasp," Richard said, sadly, as he and Penelope drove homeward. Penelope merely sighed in response.

"I did not solve the mystery as you expected and wished," he continued, taking her hand in his, "still I object to being cheated of my happiness. When are you going to marry me?"

"Oh!" Penelope tried to say in playful surprise, but her hand trembled.

" This is the tenth.   I will give you until the twenty-first to make what little preparations you   need   for   the   wedding," Richard   said, masterfully, yet tenderly.

"Oh!   If   you   talk   that   way I   suppose I must meekly obey," Penelope said, as, with a sigh of content, she allowed Dick to take her in his arms.

THE   END.

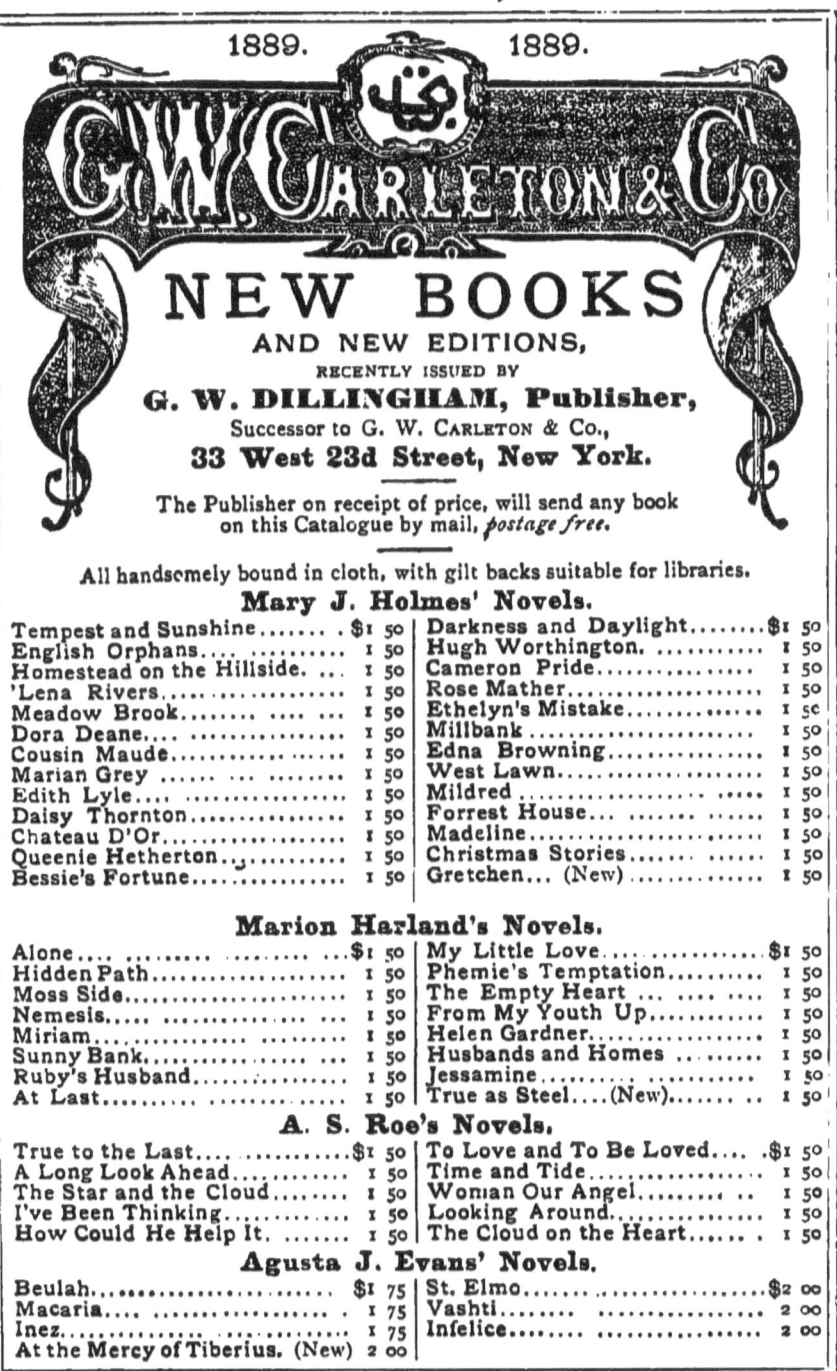

1889. 1889.

NEW BOOKS

AND NEW EDITIONS,
RECENTLY ISSUED BY

G. W. DILLINGHAM, Publisher,
Successor to G. W. CARLETON & CO.,

33 West 23d Street, New York.

The Publisher on receipt of price, will send any book
on this Catalogue by mail, *postage free.*

All handsomely bound in cloth, with gilt backs suitable for libraries.

Mary J. Holmes' Novels.

Tempest and Sunshine.......	$1 50	Darkness and Daylight........	$1 50
English Orphans....	1 50	Hugh Worthington.	1 50
Homestead on the Hillside. ...	1 50	Cameron Pride................	1 50
'Lena Rivers..................	1 50	Rose Mather..................	1 50
Meadow Brook........	1 50	Ethelyn's Mistake.............	1 5c
Dora Deane....	1 50	Millbank	1 50
Cousin Maude................	1 50	Edna Browning...............	1 50
Marian Grey	1 50	West Lawn....................	1 50
Edith Lyle....	1 50	Mildred	1 50
Daisy Thornton...............	1 50	Forrest House...	1 50
Chateau D'Or..................	1 50	Madeline.....................	1 50
Queenie Hetherton..,........	1 50	Christmas Stories......	1 50
Bessie's Fortune...............	1 50	Gretchen... (New)	1 50

Marion Harland's Novels.

Alone....	$1 50	My Little Love...............	$1 50
Hidden Path..................	1 50	Phemie's Temptation.........	1 50
Moss Side....................	1 50	The Empty Heart	1 50
Nemesis.....	1 50	From My Youth Up...........	1 50
Miriam..........	1 50	Helen Gardner...............	1 50
Sunny Bank..................	1 50	Husbands and Homes	1 50
Ruby's Husband.....,........	1 50	Jessamine.........	1 50
At Last.........	1 50	True as Steel....(New)....... ..	1 50

A. S. Roe's Novels.

True to the Last....	$1 50	To Love and To Be Loved....	$1 50
A Long Look Ahead............	1 50	Time and Tide................	1 50
The Star and the Cloud.......	1 50	Woman Our Angel......... ..	1 50
I've Been Thinking...........	1 50	Looking Around...............	1 50
How Could He Help It.	1 50	The Cloud on the Heart...... .	1 50

Agusta J. Evans' Novels.

Beulah.,..•••••••••••...••	$1 75	St. Elmo........	$2 00
Macaria....	1 75	Vashti........	2 00
Inez........................	1 75	Infelice........	2 00
At the Mercy of Tiberius. (New)	2 00		

BEST NOVELS BY BEST AUTHORS.

MADISON SQUARE SERIES.

PRICE 25 CENTS EACH.

No. 1. ALONE - - - - - By Marion Harland.
No. 2. GUY EARLSCOURT'S WIFE - - By Kay Agnes Fleming.
No. 3. TRUE AS STEEL - - - By Marion Harland.
No. 4. TEMPEST AND SUNSHINE - - By Mary J. Holmes.
No. 5. A WONDERFUL WOMAN - - By May Agnes Fleming.
No. 6. MADAME - - - - By Frank Lee Benedict.
No. 7. THE HIDDEN PATH - - - By Marion Harland.
No. 8. A TERRIBLE SECRET - - By May Agnes Fleming.
No. 9. 'LENA RIVERS - - - By Mary J. Holmes.
No. 10. WARWICK - - - - By M. T. Walworth.
No. 11. A MAD MARRIAGE - - By May Agnes Fleming.
No. 12. HOTSPUR - - - - By M. T. Walworth.
No. 13. HER FRIEND - - - By Frank Lee Benedict.
No. 14. THE ENGLISH ORPHANS - - By Mary J. Holmes.
No. 15. A WIFE'S TRAGEDY - - By May Agnes Fleming.
No. 16. DOCTOR ANTONIO - - By Ruffini.
No. 17. SUNNYBANK - - - By Marion Harland.
No. 18. HAMMER AND ANVIL - - By Frank Lee Benedict.
No. 19. MARIAN GREY - - - By Mary J. Holmes.

☞ They are the handsomest 25 cent books in the market, and sell

www.ingramcontent.com/pod-product-compliance
Lightning Source LLC
Chambersburg PA
CBHW030112030726
47498CB00007B/2357